KUTENAI KILLING

STONECROFT SAGA 12

B.N. RUNDELL

Kutenai Killing

Paperback Edition

Wolfpack Publishing
6032 Wheat Penny Avenue
Las Vegas, NV 89122

wolfpackpublishing.com

Paperback ISBN 978-1-64734-225-8
eBook ISBN 978-1-64734-224-1

KUTENAI KILLING

DEDICATION

Inspiration. That mystical element that every writer yearns for, but often has a hard time recognizing it when it comes. It is usually made evident when it flows out of the tips of fingers dancing on a keyboard, often surprising even the writer. But as I ponder inspiration, I think of people and their stories. Maybe it's the hollow ring of a voice from the past, the echo of words from nearby, or the thought that is planted when something is read or even overheard. For me, inspiration comes at odd times and in unique ways, but this I know, it's usually in the presence of my life's partner, my loving wife, Dawn, who patiently listens to every word as I read each chapter aloud for her approval. And for that, I say, thank you. Thank you to the voices of the past, the echoes of the present, the whispers of the future, and the patience of my love. Thank you.

1 / SPRING

The sky was overcast with a spring haze, thin clouds shrouded the mountain peaks, and the sun that usually strutted across the blue in the springtime, was hiding. In the clearing before the cabin, Cougar Woman and Grey Dove were enjoying the crisp mountain air as they sat watching their infants lying on their bellies, absorbing the warmth of the buffalo robe beneath them. They both had taken their fill of their mother's milk and were content as sleep closed their eyes. The big black wolf lay at the edge of the robe, his face between his paws as he watched over the two little ones.

Chipmunk, Dove's oldest child, the ever-curious toddler was carefully taking every petal of a pine cone off the stem, and with sticky fingers, he tried to shake it free. Failing, he stretched out nature's toy for his mother to pluck if from his fingers. As she did, she noticed Cougar Woman lean to the side, looking overhead as she reached for her bow and quiver that lay beside her. Cougar quickly came to her feet, nocking an arrow as she rose. The expression on Cougar Woman's face made Dove catch her breath and she leaned out from under the long branches of the ponderosa, looking upward for whatever had alarmed her friend. Cougar stepped from under the overhanging limbs of the tall pine, every move, deliberate and measured, holding the bow before her, looking skyward. High above, a majestic golden eagle soared in a wide circle, wings outspread and unmoving, taking its lift from the updraft. It seemed so peaceful and harmless, floating on the cool air. Then it dropped his head downward and let out its high-pitched scream, the sound that would cause potential prey to scamper for cover, the movement revealing their whereabouts. Cougar glanced at the two dozing infants, saw Bobcat roll to his side, stretching his pudgy arm up as if reaching for his mother. Cougar turned wide-eyed to look at the eagle. Its wide soaring circle changed, its head bobbed and once in position, it prepared to dive. The proven warrior was confident as she took aim, holding her breath, knowing the cost of failure.

Dove jumped to her feet, looked high above to see the golden eagle soaring on the cool updraft, wings spread and head searching the ground below. With one hand to shade her eyes, she glanced from the eagle to the children, saw Chipmunk was occupied with another cone and was near the trunk of the tree, unseen by the bird of prey. As she looked back, the big eagle had tucked his wings to the side and started his plummeting descent. Dove looked at Cougar, glanced at Wolf who came to his feet, head back and looking at the diving demon of death. Cougar lifted her bow, and in an instant, brought the weapon to full draw, took aim, and let the arrow fly. With an eagle's descent reaching over a hundred miles an hour, the flying target would be difficult, if not impossible to hit.

Wolf rocked back on his hind legs, fangs showing from his open mouth, eyes flaring orange, a raspy growl coming from deep in his chest. He saw the arrow fly, kept his eyes on the brown predator and lunged. The big wolf's timing was perfect, his mouth catching the forward edge of the eagle's wing, just as it fluttered from the impact of the arrow. As the big wolf lunged, Dove leaped across the infants, shielding them with her body.

The impact of the wolf against the huge bird, carried it out of its trajectory and Wolf and eagle landed in a flurry of feathers as the big beast growled and shook the bird side to side. He spat out the mouthful of broken feathers, saw the bird flap a broken wing, then grabbed it by the throat and ripped the head from the body. Again, he spat feathers and shook his head trying to rid himself of the fluffy plumage.

Wolf stood over the carnage, head down and watching as his front paws were spread wide, but the only movement was the flutter of down from the breeze that whispered through the pines. Cougar, took a deep breath, steadied herself and went to Wolf's side, dropped to one knee beside him and ran her fingers through the scruff of his neck, "We make a good team, boy!" She turned to look back at Dove, who sat up, lifting her little girl, Squirrel to her chest. She reached down with her free hand and stroked the back of Bobcat, the only child of Cougar Woman and Gabe. A quick glance back to the tree showed Chipmunk busy with another cone, eagerly tearing it apart, unmoved by the excitement.

Cougar smiled back at Dove, picked up the carcass of the eagle and walked toward the cabin, deposited the feathery pile on the porch and returned to the buffalo robe. They would pluck the feathers and down and remove the talons. After stripping the carcass, the fine bones would be sorted and dried and used, some for decoration, some for other purposes. It was not in their nature to waste any part of an animal taken for either food or in defense of the family.

Cougar put a hand at her back, leaned backwards just a mite, grimaced, and waddled back to the buffalo robe to fetch her one-year old son, Bobcat. She dropped to one knee and reached out for the boy, who looked at his mother wide-eyed and Cougar struggled to pick up the plump boy, lifting him over her swollen belly, groaning as she did. She shook her head and grinned as she looked at Dove, who shook her head as she said, "You should not lift him when you are like that. You will make the baby come soon!"

"I am ready to have the little one in my arms instead of here," nodding to her stretched tunic that did little for support.

"He will come when he is ready!" declared Dove, as she rocked her little girl back to sleep.

"I think you are right, it is a boy," replied Cougar, rubbing her belly with her free hand as she cradled the infant in the crook of her arm. The women stood and turned to the cabin, strolling close to the trees, lifting their heads to take in the scents of spring. The musky smell of the white barked aspen as the fresh buds pushed their way through the thick red folds, the tang of the pines as fresh needles made their entrance at the end of each branch, and the hint of some early flowers that forced their way past the dirtied crystals of left over snow, eager to show their spring colors and light fragrances. It was a time of renewal, refreshing in color and scents, the cool breeze chasing away the stuffiness of closed-up havens and a shuttered cabin. But it was dry, drier than usual. The winter had started early and came like a banshee, blowing and blustering with blizzard after blizzard, piling and drifting snow in the deep woods and across the flats. But after about four months of hard winter, it was as if spring came early. In late January, the snow began to melt and runoff flooded the river, spreading water across the valley bottom, but the thirsty land soaked it up and by late February, warmer temperatures became the norm. Trees started budding and sprouting early, but when no moisture came, pine needles grew brittle, aspen buds dried up and the few leaves that forced their way past the dry crust of red buds, were wrinkled and dry. Even now, when cool winds would demand jackets or blankets, bare arms and legs gave the feeling of mid-summer, and it was just mid-April.

Dove glanced at the position of the sun, “The men will return soon, if they do not have trouble, like last year.”

Cougar grinned, shook her head, “I remember the mule fought off that wolf pack!”

“But not before we lost a horse!” responded Cougar and both women turned at the sound of approaching horses, hooves clattering on the rocky trail from below, but the men would be returning from the upper pasture, not the lower trail. Cougar slipped another arrow from the quiver and stepped in front of Dove, motioning her to the cabin. She stood, feet apart, bow held low before her, as she watched the opening in the trees that would show any visitor’s approach. She smiled as she recognized the oldest son of Spotted Eagle, the war leader of the Salish people whose winter camp was at the upper end of the basin. Red Hawk lifted his hand in greeting as he and another rode into the clearing. The second young man looked familiar to Cougar, but she could not remember his name.

"Red Hawk! It is good to see you again, step down." She looked at the other young man, motioned for him to step down as well.

"Cougar Woman, it is good to see you." He turned to his companion, "You remember Beaver, the son of our Shaman, Raven's Wing."

Cougar looked to Red Hawk's friend, smiled and nodded, "It has been a long time, Beaver. Welcome." She looked at Red Hawk, "And what brings you to our home?"

"Is Spirit Bear here?" he asked, dodging the question. "My father said I was to speak to him."

Cougar smiled, "He will return soon. He and Black Buffalo are bringing the horses down from the upper meadow. You can wait at the corral, or you can come inside."

Red Hawk glanced at his friend, then turned back to Cougar, "We will wait at the corral. Beaver has never been here and I will show him around," and paused, then added, "If it pleases you."

"That will be fine. Take your horses for water at the stream that comes from the corral."

The small herd of horses crowded down the trail that led from the upper pasture where the herd had been grazing since the weather turned spring like. Gabe, aboard his black Andalusian stallion, Ebony, led the herd, and Ezra, aboard his long-legged bay gelding, pushed the band along. The only mule lagged behind the rest of the animals and delighted in aggravating Ezra as he would stop and grab a mouthful of grass at every opportunity, but would eventually relent to Ezra's prodding usually after laying his ears back and threatening to bite anything that came near. The others, a spotted rump appaloosa mare, her yearling colt that was almost a mirror image, a pair of buckskins, one gelding and a mare, a steeldust mustang gelding, a big grey gelding and Cougar Woman's strawberry roan gelding, made up the rest of the small herd.

As the bunch broke from the trees, Gabe leaned down and swung the pole gate wide open, watching the rest of the animals crowd into the big corral, although it would be better described as a fenced meadow that covered about five acres of grass with a little creek running through the middle. Ezra followed the bunch through, reined up as Gabe shut the gate and they rode to the lower end where the tack shed, lean-to shelter, and cabin lay near the tall cliff face of the timbered hillside. They saw two unfamiliar figures standing at the gate, but when

Red Hawk lifted his hand high, Gabe squinted and recognized the young man. He turned to Ezra, "That's Red Hawk, Spotted Eagle's boy."

"Hmmm, wonder what brings them down thisaway at this time o' year?"

"Reckon we'll find out soon 'nuff!"

2 / INVITE

Gabriel Stonecroft and Ezra Blackwell had been friends since childhood and spent most of their time exploring the woods outside of Philadelphia, honing the skills that would be needed if they ever got to fulfill their dream of exploring the western wilderness. And now, that dream fulfilled, they were living with their Shoshone wives and their children in the foothills of the Bitterroot mountains in what had been French Louisiana, but was now known as Spanish Louisiana, or by most just as Louisiana territory. The men had left Philadelphia after an unfortunate outcome of a duel between Gabe and the son of a well-connected member of Philadelphia society, who placed a bounty on Gabe's head for retribution for killing his son in the duel.

After several years exploring the eastern plains between the Mississippi river and the Rocky Mountains, the men found themselves at home in the mountains and had befriended several of the native tribes and explored the wild country at will. The cabin where the women waited, was built two summers ago and had been the birthplace of Ezra's youngest child, Squirrel, and Gabe's only child, Bobcat. And would probably see the birthing of Gabe and Cougar Woman's second child, due any day.

The men rode to the gate in the pole fence where the two visitors waited and stepped down to strip the gear from their horses. Gabe spoke to Red Hawk, "So, how is the best horse trainer of the Salish doing with those yearlings?"

"They are doing well! They have good spirits and learn quickly!" declared a grinning Red Hawk. He had been entrusted with the training of three colts sired by Gabe's big Andalusian out of the mare's that were the pride of his father, Spotted Eagle.

"Good, good! I knew you could do it. And how is your father and his new bride doing?"

"My father sent us to speak to you," declared the now somber young man.

Gabe noted the change in his manner and stopped what he was doing and stepped closer to the fence. He put his foot on the bottom rail, and looked over the top rail at the young man and asked, "What is it?"

Red Hawk took a deep breath and began, "Our people will leave soon for our summer encampment in the north." He glanced around at the meadow grasses and the trees, "The winter was hard on the land and there is little graze for the animals. My father is concerned about his horses and thought of you. He asks if you and your family would like to join with our people and come north to the summer encampment."

Gabe glanced at Ezra, frowning slightly, then turned back to Red Hawk, "What your father says is true. This land is very dry and it does not look good." He reached down and plucked a handful of grass, put it between his palms and rubbed them together, turning the dry grass into crumbly stubble. He looked at Ezra, "And when things are this dry, there is always the danger of fire."

Gabe looked back at Red Hawk, "We'll finish with the horses. You and . . ." he looked at the other young man and frowned, "You're Beaver, aren't you?"

"Yes, I am Beaver," answered a smiling young man, pleased he was remembered by the great Spirit Bear, the name Gabe was known by among the natives.

He glanced at Red Hawk, "You two go on to the cabin. The women are prob'ly fixin' somethin' to eat, and we'll be along shortly."

The boys grinned and turned away to return to the front of the cabin. Gabe went to Ebony, and finished stripping off the saddle and hackamore, and asked, "What do you think?"

Ezra frowned, “You mean about the invite?”

“Yeah. I been looking at everything this morning and it doesn’t look good. If we don’t get some moisture soon, everything’s gonna be brown and dead ‘fore long.”

“Looks thataway, don’t it. But leavin’ everything and goin’ north for the summer? And you and Cougar with a newborn? I dunno.”

“Guess we’ll need to talk it over with the women, ya’ reckon?”

“Might be best,” resolved Ezra, grinning.

As they mounted the steps, the men looked at the pile of fluff and feathers, frowned at one another and stepped through the doorway. Gabe saw Cougar Woman standing before the fire, stirring something in the hanging pot, then turn to smile at her man. He asked, “What’s all the feathers on the porch?”

“An eagle,” she answered, stoically.

Gabe glanced from her to Dove, then Ezra, and back. “What’d he do? Just fall out of the sky and land on our porch?”

“Wolf,” she said, as she turned back to the pot.

Gabe shrugged, shook his head slightly, and went to the table to pour a cup of coffee. Ezra joined him and they sat, looking at one another and grinning. Ezra spoke to the room, “So, they told you!”

Both women turned to stare at Ezra, then turned

back to their doings. The two young men joined the men at the table as Red Hawk asked, "What will you do?"

"Dunno, Hawk. Reckon we'll have to wait until the women are in a more talkative mood," suggested Gabe, sipping at the hot coffee that steamed from the cup. He looked at Hawk, "When's the village gonna move?"

"One hand of days."

"And how long does it take to get to this summer camp?" asked Ezra.

"Two hands of days," answered Red Hawk, nodding as he spoke. His excitement about the coming journey north was evident in the eyes of both the young men as they often looked to one another and found it difficult to sit still.

"Tell me about your summer encampment, what's the country like?" asked Gabe.

"There is a big lake, so big you cannot see one end from the other. There is land in the lake, with trees and more. The biggest has wild horses! We are going to go to that place and capture some horses!" declared Red Hawk, glancing to his friend and both boys nodding exuberantly.

"What about the land around the lake? Flat, dry, mountains?"

"Hills, mountains, trees, meadows, it is a beautiful land, but the winters are hard, so we come here for the cold season."

As they spoke, Gabe glanced at Cougar Woman often, noticing she was leaning against the side of the fireplace, one arm extended to support her as she stirred. It was not a normal stance for his woman, she seldom leaned on anything. He looked back to the table and lifted his cup, but as he brought it to his mouth, he heard a muffled grunt come from Cougar and he quickly turned to see her drop to her knees.

"Dove!" he shouted as he came to his feet, "It's Cougar!" he added as he dropped to his knees beside her. She twisted around to look at her man, grimacing with pain, then looked up at Dove. Gabe looked from Cougar to Dove and instantly knew the women did not need him near. He stepped out of the way of Dove, let her help Cougar to her feet, and the two went to the bedroom and shut the door. Gabe stood staring at the closed door, scarcely breathing, then slowly turned to the men at the table. "We need to go outside. Grab the plates and such, Ezra. I'll get the pot. Red Hawk, you take the coffeepot and Beaver, you grab the cups. It might be a while."

As they started to leave, the door to the bedroom opened just a mite and Dove called out, "Ezra, take the little ones!"

Ezra looked at Gabe, nodded, and quickly took the wooden plates and utensils to the porch and both men returned for the three little ones. Ezra grabbed the buffalo robe in one hand, ushered Chipmunk before him as he carried Squirrel. Gabe lifted Bobcat to his hip and they stepped outside.

Choosing the sunshine over the shady porch, the robe was spread, and the children sat down, to be joined by the men. Gabe did the honors of serving up the stew and the men sat around the blanket, cross-legged, and ate. With a few glances to one another, no conversation rose, just the sounds of utensils scraping against the wooden trenchers, and the sounds of men enjoying a good meal.

Once finished with the meal, the men sat about talking horses, hunting and adventures, as older men are wont to do with impressionable young men and to pass the time as Gabe was worried about Cougar Woman and the birthing. But the little ones kept their minds and hands busy, just keeping up with the rambunctious youngsters. Chipmunk was quick on his feet and gave Ezra a workout keeping after him. And the little ones, Bobcat and Squirrel, were kept busy with a pair of eagle feathers. Gabe bribed Red Hawk and Beaver into plucking the eagle carcass by offering a pair of tail feathers to each one. The tail feathers of the golden eagle were especially treasured among the native people and used to show honors and deeds of bravery and were earned in battle. Red Hawk had earned his first feather but would treasure the new feathers in anticipation of greater honors. Beaver was still looking forward to earning his feather, hoping the summer would not pass before he could earn the honor of his first feather and be called a warrior of the people.

Gabe and Ezra talked about the possibility of going north with the Salish and agreed it would be a smart thing to do, since the probability of a drought threatened. But they would not make the trip if it would be too difficult for the women and the children, especially with the new one.

Gabe spoke to Red Hawk, "Tell your father that we will probably join you, but not to wait for us. With the little one," nodding his head to the cabin, "we might wait a little longer before we start out."

Red Hawk grinned broadly and motioned for Beaver to fetch the horses. "It is good. You will see that our summer camp is a good place with lots of grass and water. Perhaps you too could capture some of the wild horses!"

"Perhaps, but for now, we have enough horses for our needs, maybe too many!"

The boys mounted up and with a high-handed wave, they started their almost two-day journey back to their village. Gabe looked at Ezra, "Whatchu think?"

"That's all we can do. We're not going anywhere without the women, not since our last episode with the Paiute and I wouldn't want to anyway. I reckon it'll be up to Coyote Woman and what she thinks she can handle, but if I know her, ain't nothin' gonna slow her down!"

Gabe chuckled, thinking back to the time he first met her, and how surprised he was that she was a warrior and a war leader with her people, the Tukku-tikka Shoshone, and had repeatedly proven she was a woman to ride beside her man. The birth of their first child, just over a year past, did not slow her, and he believed it would be the same this time around, but he also acknowledged his limitation concerning the ways of women. He grinned, glanced to Ezra and said, "Prob'ly not, and I wouldn't want to be the one to suggest such a thing!"

3 / NEWCOMER

The newborn was at his mother's breast when Gabe was finally allowed into the bedroom. He kissed Cougar, lightly stroked the top of the newborn's head and sat on the edge of the bed near Cougar's knees. "Dove tells me we have another boy!" declared Gabe, grinning proudly.

"Yes, a hungry boy!" responded Cougar.

"You alright?"

"Yes, of course. It is the way of things, I will help Dove with the meal as soon as your son is done," she replied, smiling down at the warm bundle on her chest.

The door opened and the rest of the extended family came storming in, led by Ezra and Dove, who had Squirrel in one arm and Bobcat in the other. Chipmunk sat on the edge of the bed beside Gabe and looked at the little one, glanced up at his daddy, Ezra, and asked, "Why is he red?"

"That's because he's like a fox! You know, those red things with the big tails you like to chase through the woods but can never catch."

"They are not red like that!" nodding toward the new addition.

"Well, maybe we'll just have to name him Fox and see if he turns red like them!"

The boy grinned, nodding, and looked back at the baby. "He's littler than a fox!"

Cougar swung aboard her strawberry roan, settled into her saddle and checked on Fox in the cradleboard that hung from the pommel beside her right leg. She had handed off Bobcat to his daddy and glanced over to see the boy seated on the saddle in front of Gabe, making it a tight fit for both. Ezra had Chipmunk seated before him and Dove had Squirrel still in a cradleboard. Although Cougar had a board for Bobcat, Gabe suggested he try the boy with him and would put him in the cradleboard if it became uncomfortable for either.

They had waited a week before starting out after the Salish village, that was now on the move to their summer encampment far to the north, but Gabe was unconcerned and knew they would catch up before the villagers reached their summer camp. He looked back at the string of horses that trailed behind them, tethered together, and lined out. Ezra trailed the buckskin gelding that was harnessed with the travois that carried Dove's tipi. The mule and big grey were packed, but allowed to follow free rein, while Gabe led the Appaloosa mare and the steeldust mustang on a long lead and the Appy's colt trotted freely beside his mother. It was quite a group and was a miniature company of the Salish village as they had many travois, a sizeable herd of horses, and many riders.

It was familiar country and trail. Spotted Eagle had told them last spring that this was the route taken by his people when they went to the summer camp and it was the same trail they followed last summer to take Two Drums, the young Nez Percé they freed from the Blackfoot, back to his people. By the end of the second day, they had traversed the hills behind the usual Salish camp and dropped into the valley of the headwaters of the Bitterroot river. The valley was bordered on the east by many barren finger ridges that extended from a long range of low mountains that ran north and south. On the west edge were the sawtooth peaks of the Bitterroot range, a long line of granite tipped peaks that lifted their heads high above timberline and held snow most of the year, but even the Bitterroots were sparse with the snow cover. They made camp at the confluence of the Bitterroot river, now but a small mountain run-off creek and another even smaller creek. It was a grassy valley and the grass here was fresh and green, well-watered by the runoff from the high mountains.

Making camp had already fallen into a routine, even with this only being the second night on their journey. Gabe and Ezra tended the animals, the women started the fire and the meal and when the men returned, the children were quickly handed off and the women, smiling, busied themselves with the meal.

For the next three days, they traveled familiar trails, the trail they followed on their return from the Coeur D'Alene village. They made good time, the horses and children traveled well and by the end of the fifth day on the trail, they chose to take some extra time in camp. They were on the north bank of the confluence of the three rivers where the Bitterroot river came from a smaller valley into a broad and fertile land. They crossed the river and chose a site in the tall cottonwoods with a wide meadow of tall green grass to the north. With the horses picketed on long lines, yet close to the water, the family stretched out on the grass knoll for a brief rest before starting the evening meal.

Across the river and behind their camp to the southwest, the rugged timber covered foothills marked the north end of the Bitterroot range. It was rough and dense country, but still the land of the Salish while across these mountains, the many tribes of the northwest made their homes. The Nez Percé, Coeur

D'Alene, the Kalispel and further north, the Kutenai, all made those mountains their homes and all were friendly with the Salish, or at least not enemies. But where they were bound was almost due north, into a new land to Gabe and company, but ancestral lands of the Salish.

Gabe commented, "I can already tell the difference between this land and that back by the cabin. Not nearly as dry here!"

"And if it stays like this, the further north we go, the better it'll get!" answered Ezra, laying back in the grass, his fingers locked behind his head as he watched the few clouds move slowly across the late afternoon sky.

"There are Blackfoot!" declared Cougar Woman, not as a warning but a caution of what could happen.

Gabe chuckled, "There are always Blackfoot! But isn't their land further east from here?"

"Yes, but not so far." She sat up and motioned to the east, "Their land is beyond those mountains, but they never let those mountains stop them from raiding what they think is a weaker enemy."

They had dealt with Blackfoot many times before and knew them as a dreaded and fearful enemy, ferocious in battle and vicious in dealing with their enemies. But they were not his immediate concern, with the Salish near, most raiding parties would shy away from such a band with many warriors. Gabe knew they were only a day behind the Salish, it was evident by the multitude of tracks and sign they followed and decided it would be good to take some time to rest the animals and get some fresh meat before continuing.

Gabe sat up, looking around at the lush land that lay between the winding river and the foothills to the northeast, the route taken by Spotted Eagle and his people. To his left, the big river flowed north, and from the east came the two smaller rivers that joined the Bitterroot River as it came from the mountains to the south.

Gabe nodded toward the smaller rivers and the grassy marshland that lay between the two, and to the north extending into the grassy meadow. "I'm thinkin' that might be good for some deer, maybe even a moose." He paused, glanced at Ezra, "But if you're committed to fish, you can do some fishin' while I do some huntin'."

Ezra jumped to his feet, looked down at Gabe, "I do believe some fresh trout would be mighty tasty," and he looked at the women, "don't you ladies?"

Dove smiled, "Yes, but some deer meat would be good to fry up for our morning meal."

Ezra looked back at Gabe, "Guess we got it to do!" and started for the gear to fetch his fishing tackle.

With an early start and full bellies, everyone was glad to be back on the trail, everyone except Bobcat who complained about the tight fit between his father and the pommel of the saddle, but Gabe folded a blanket under him and let him stretch his legs on either side of the saddle horn, resting them on the pommel, and he was happy. With just an hour on the trail, headed almost due north, they came to the mouth of the break between the low-lying barren hills that pointed them toward the timberland that blanketed the higher hills to the north. It was a deep cut between two steep and heavily timbered hills that held tall ponderosa and fir trees that crowded together to blacken the hills. But within about three miles, the foothills lay back and opened to a dog-leg valley that bent to the west and shadowed a long finger ridge with slopes that bore little else besides bunch grass and cacti.

As they rode the bottom of the valley, staying on the south of a small and shallow river that held thick cottonwoods and a few maple and oak which afforded ample cover, the tall mountains that formed a north-south line stood watch from afar. Gabe leaned over to look at the tracks of the Salish, sat up and looked at the others, "I reckon we're just a few hours behind 'em, maybe a little more."

"So, we could catch up 'fore nightfall?" suggested Ezra.

"Maybe, we'll see."

It was a good day of travel, clear skies, warm sunshine, and eager horses, and they made good time, making the cut at the end of the long ridge by late afternoon. The trail bent through the snake of a valley between the low buttes, then broke into the open and the huge basin that lay west of the tall peaks and stretched to the Salish River that bordered the basin some fourteen to fifteen miles west. The range of bald knobs to the west shaded the setting sun, as they decided to camp below a small catchwater pond. The tracks of the Salish bent around the knob and they were probably within ten miles or so, but they were tired and the children were getting a little cranky and the women said, "It is time to make camp."

Gabe glanced at Ezra, then to Cougar Woman and said, "Sounds good!"

4 / BLACKFOOT

Red Crow sat in the darkness, glaring at the many dancers that moved with the rhythm of the big drum that rested in the middle of the circle. The warriors sat around the big drum, chanting as they beat the buffalo hide stretched taut over the frame. Many couples danced to the beat and shuffled around the circle, strutting in their finest attire. Beaded and fringed dresses were decorated with elks' teeth and feathers, fans of feathers waved above their heads and roaches swayed with the movements. It was a joyous time for the *Niitsitapi* or Blackfoot people for the *Okan* or Sun Dance was completed and this was the Grass Dance when everyone could join.

The gathering of bands of the Piikáni people for the prayerful Sun Dance was not just for the blood offering of the dance, but to celebrate the rebirth of all things at this time of year and to join with those that were from other bands. It was also a time for young people to find a mate and be joined in marriage. Red Crow had long believed his woman would be The Feather, the beautiful daughter of the leader of their Big Pipes band, Two Bulls. Although Red Crow had proven himself as a warrior and leader and had been chosen as one of two war leaders, The Feather, who had been his friend since they were youths, had recently shown more attention to White Eagle, the other war leader and Red Crow's long-time archrival.

Red Crow glowered at the two that danced with hands joined and smiling and laughing at one another. White Eagle's father, Lame Horse, was the Shaman of the Big Pipes band and the confidant and counsel to the leader, Two Bulls. White Eagle had been studying under his father and was becoming a respected Shaman in his own right, but he had not chosen his path yet. As a war leader, he could one day become the leader or chief of his own band, but as a Shaman, he would also be a respected leader, but not with the power of a chief.

Red Crow and White Eagle had an ongoing adversarial relationship that had begun when they were boys with their first weapons and had competed against one another in all the games of childhood and all the contests of their youth. Neither had continually proven themselves the better, but the animosity had festered until now Red Crow had replaced any friendship with hatred and envy. And to have White Eagle dancing with the woman he had believed would be his wife, raised his ire further still. Red Crow looked at the man beside him, Weasel Horse, "I will kill him!" he snarled as he slammed his fist into his palm. His nostrils flared and his eyes squinted as he breathed deep, his chest lifting and falling with anger.

"You cannot do that! You will be banned, become a renegade!" answered Weasel Horse.

"I will stand over his body, cut off his hands and his feet and more! He will have nothing on the other side! He will always know I have destroyed him!" grumbled the war leader.

"It would be better if you take the woman from him, that will kill him here!" declared Weasel Horse, slamming his fist against his chest.

Crow turned to face his friend, "How? She dances with him now! That tells everyone they are together!"

"But she does not decide that! Two Bulls decides! If you have better gifts, more horses and prizes taken in battle, *You* will get her as your woman!"

Crow glared, turned back to watch the dancers, glanced back at Weasel, "Yes!" As he stared at the people of the Piikáni, he considered the suggestion of his friend and his eyes slowly dropped into slits and his upper lip curled upwards as he considered, then with a slow nod, he turned to Weasel, "Go, now, tell the warriors of the Horn Society we leave at first light! We go to raid the Salish and the Kutenai and take their horses and more!"

White Eagle saw the raiding party leave at first light, even though he had not been told of the raid, he knew Red Crow was in the lead. Eagle grinned as he stepped from his lodge, seeing the dust rise from the heels of the last horse of the raiders. He knew what Red Crow was planning. After his time with The Feather at the Grass Dance, White Eagle knew Red Crow would try something to win her back and the only possibility he had would be to lead a raid and return with many horses to pay the bride price for The Feather. But her father could choose to accept or demand more payment, or a payment of different value.

White Eagle saw one of the warriors of the Lance society, Elk Child and motioned him over. "Go, gather the warriors. First, learn where Red Crow goes, then tell the others. Where he goes, we will do more. We will go on a raid to count many coups and take many horses and captives!" Elk Child nodded and left at a trot to assemble the other warriors for the raid spoken of by White Eagle. It would be a raid that would bring many honors and more for all the warriors, for any raid led by White Eagle would enrich his people.

It was a three-day ride from the camp of the Piikáni to the valley of the Salish Lake. They camped at the edge of the trees below a shallow lake that lay in the cut between the high peaks and a basin of foothills. As they started into the flats at the break of day, Red Crow stopped them when he saw movement and dust at the edge of the long line of foothills that bordered the south edge of the valley. He knew the saddle crossing where the dust rose and suspected it to be the big band of Salish coming to their summer grounds. He turned back to the men, "Crazy Dog, you and Black Snake, go! You see who that is, return soon!" as he pointed to the wispy dust cloud across the valley bottom. As he watched the two take to the trees, he motioned the others to follow. They would stay within tree cover to cross the lower end of the big basin and although it would be a circuitous route, it would prevent being seen by any of the Salish or others.

The scouts returned and within the hour, Red Crow led his men across the trail taken by the Salish. They stayed to the south of the feeder creek that flowed east to west across the southern end of the big basin. The sign of the Salish showed they had continued north across the flatlands directly toward the big lake. But Red Crow knew the land and had planned his approach, choosing to use the dog leg ridge of buttes that pointed north along the west edge of the basin and would take them nearer the encampment of the

Salish. Near the point of that long ridge, the Salish river began to carve its way around the west edge of the basin right after its confluence with the narrow creek known as Crow Creek.

Another island of buttes stretched northward just beyond the solitary round butte that stood as a sentinel in the middle of the broad grassy basin. The series of buttes and ridges would offer Red Crow and his men ample cover to approach the encampment of the Salish, but he thought as they followed the small feeder creek, turned to Weasel Horse, "When we come to the Salish river, we will wait until dark before going closer to the camp. Until then, you and Crazy Dog will scout the horse herd. The Salish like to put the horses out on the big island, but we can take it from them in the night. They will be tired and lazy; the guards will be young and sleepy. It will be an easy raid!"

Elk Child rode beside his friend, White Eagle, and asked, "Do we follow Red Crow to join him in his raid?"

Eagle grinned, shook his head, "No, we follow to make him think we will join in his raid, but we will make our own raid. We will come to the valley of the Salish Lake soon, but we will go north. Red Crow thinks he can raid the Salish, but they keep their horses on the big island and no one can take them from the island without the people knowing. We will make our raid on the Kutenai. Their herd is smaller but can be taken easily. And they have women and other things that will be great honor for our young warriors. It takes a real warrior to count coups and return unharmed and the things taken from an enemy will be honors for many."

"When Crow and his men return, bloodied and shamed, defeated with no coups or captives, he will be like the dog he is with his tail between his legs. You will see and the people will sing songs about us!"

As they broke from the trees, the sun was laying low on the distant mountains. Golden lances stretched high into the fading blue sky and the land showed the hint of color as the blanket of sunset lay across the flats. The long line of granite peaks marched northward, helmeted soldiers guarding the eastern edge of the Salish basin and lake, with the wide dark green, almost black, of the timbered tunic stretching from timberline down the shoulders to flank the flats. White Eagle spoke to his men, "Lynx Killer, Calf Shirt, scout!" he waved his arm to the north toward the dim trail that stayed just inside the tree line.

Eagle looked to Elk Child, nodded toward the grassy meadow that lay below the towering timber of fir and ponderosa, "We will camp there, leave at first light."

Elk Child quickly directed the sixteen other warriors as they arrayed their camp in the deepening shadows of the tall trees, picketing the horses, picking their sites for their blankets, and more. This would be a cold camp for they were now within sight of their prey and until their raids were finished, there would be no fires for warmth or food. Elk Child watched as the men settled in, proud of the younger men who were anxious to prove themselves and careful to show their skills, hard-earned though they were, but necessary for survival for a warrior of the Piikáni, Piegan Blackfoot. Each man lost in his own visions and thoughts of what great honors they would earn, what bravery they would show and what coups they would count.

Elk Child returned to the side of his friend and leader, White Eagle, sat on his haunches and nodded, "They will do well. We have many proven warriors and the others are anxious to earn the honors that will make them respected warriors of the people. They will do well," he nodded, glancing at his friend.

5 / BASIN

The grass lands stretched endlessly to the north in a wide expanse framed by the tall mountains on the east and the long rolling foothills on the west. It was an inviting and fertile plain with tall grass moving like waves of the sea stirred by the early morning breeze. After the drought plagued land to the south from whence they came, it was a veritable Eden that lay before them, inviting them onward. The grey line that silhouetted the eastern mountains pushed away the dark sky of night and the crisp air made the riders hunker down in their capotes, wrapping the little ones in the warmth as they sat before them.

Both Gabe and Ezra had their firstborns seated behind the pommels of their saddles and had opened their capotes to keep them warm from the chill and Gabe, in the lead, looked to the east to the promise of the rising sun. Pink and pale orange painted the underbellies of the few clouds and gave the peaks a faint tint of color and Gabe's eyes took in the same tint on the right shoulders of both horses and riders. He let a slow smile split his face, enjoying the leisurely ride of the morning, until Ezra spoke, "Whoa up there!"

Gabe reined up, looked back at Ezra, and saw his friend pointing to the freshly trod trail before them. The sun was well up when they broke from the cut between the hills into the open basin, as they followed the unmistakable trail of the band of Salish, a trail marked by the many travois, horses, and moccasin prints of the people. It had been a wide and in places, even churned up trail as the many villagers transported their goods on pack horses and travois. But there was something different, and the difference brought a frown from Gabe as Ezra had already stepped down and walked past the others to examine the tracks. Gabe quickly joined him. They knelt on one knee and reached down to examine the tracks, then stood and walked forward, eyes to the ground, frowning and taking in every track and sign. Gabe looked at Ezra, "What do you make of it?"

Ezra stood and motioned to the wider trail, pointing to the north, "That's the trail of the villagers, they're bound directly north, moving at a normal pace, nothing alarming." He paused, dropped his eyes to the other sign, "But this, this is a different bunch. I make it out to be a hunting party, maybe a war party. I reckon about eighteen, twenty, riders. No travois, no walkers, so it's not a village or family. And I'm thinkin' it's a war party, and since it came from the mountains yonder, that's where Cougar said the Blackfoot are and that would make this bunch," pointing at the crossing tracks, "to be a Blackfoot war party."

"And they didn't follow the Salish, so they're probably plannin' on circlin' around," he pointed to the west, moved his arm in a wide sweep to the north, "and hittin' 'em later." Gabe looked back at Ezra, then up at Cougar and Dove who had pushed their horses closer to see what concerned their men.

"Those are Blackfoot!" commented Cougar, spitting the words as if they left a bad taste in her mouth. The Blackfoot had been enemies of her people and enemies of most of the tribes west of their territory. They were the first plains Indians to get rifles from the French traders of the Hudson's Bay company and the white man's weapons gave them an advantage over their neighbors from whom they regularly stole horses and women in the many raids during the warm weather months.

Gabe looked at Cougar, "You know this country and you know the trail; do we have time to catch up to Spotted Eagle and his people to warn them?"

Cougar glanced down at the tracks, looked up at Ezra, "How many?"

"I make it to be about eighteen to twenty."

Cougar looked at the sun, its brightness almost blinding and shaded her eyes as she looked north into the wide basin. "It is a long ride to where they will camp. If we keep riding, it will be well after dark before we get there. I do not believe the Blackfoot will attack on tired horses, even if they get there before dark. They will either attack at first light tomorrow, or sometime later. The Salish put their horses on the big island and it would be hard for any raiders to get to them and take them without first attacking the village. With only two double hands of warriors against the big village of the Salish, they have some other plan. I do not know what they will do."

Ezra looked from Cougar to Gabe, shrugged as if asking a question and Gabe responded, "Sounds to me like the only thing we can do is push on and try to get to 'em 'fore the Blackfoot do and then the problem is up to Spotted Eagle and Plenty Bears." Ezra nodded and both men returned to their horses, climbed aboard behind their sons and once again wrapped the boys in their capotes and started north, following the sign of the villagers.

Dusk had lowered the curtain on the day when they sighted the village. As Spotted Eagle had described, beyond the Salish River and across a broad flat, a low ridge of timbered hills pointed north to the water bordering a lowland on the west and a smaller series of knob hills with thick timber paralleled on the east edge forming a long basin with tall ponderosa and fir giving shelter to the many tipis and families. A spit of land that pushed into the deep blue of the lake that was deep in grass held most of the lodges, the thirty or so that made up the bulk of the village.

A few had tucked their hide lodges into the tall trees for a little seclusion and protection from the cold wind that often howled off the water. Gabe reined up and sat looking around in the dim light, taking in the beauty of God's creation all around. At their feet was a wide stretch of spring flowers, blue flax and larkspur, to the side were some tall loco weed with purple blooms, all closing their petals for the night. To their right, the expansive lake stretched into the darkness but the grass before them moved like the waves of water as the breath of the creator whispered past. They had crossed the river in the last light and now sat atop the slight shoulder that came from the eastern knob hills and the campfires came to life to light their way into the village.

Red Hawk spotted them as they drew near and quickly rode to their side, "We have been looking for you! Spotted Eagle said you would come sooner, but I am glad you are here now!" declared the enthusiastic young man. He had grown some in the last year and now was more of a man and had proven himself a good hunter and warrior, but they still thought of him as the boy that spent the winter with them in the cabin after the Blackfoot raid.

Hawk pulled his horse's head around and gigged him alongside Gabe, pointing to the edge of the trees above the camp, "There is a good place there for you to camp. Away from the others and in the trees and a little spring nearby for fresh water so you do not have to carry it from the lake. Spotted Eagle said you should camp there."

Gabe grinned at the eager young man, "Sounds fine to me," then looked over to Cougar Woman for her approval of the camp. She nodded and followed Ezra and Dove to the campsite. It was a small clearing on a slight shoulder, shielded on three sides with thick timber and a sparse line of ponderosa saplings and tall trees separating the clearing from the village. The little spring had a small pool no more than a yard across and the trickle of water worked its way toward the village. Red Hawk pitched in and helped strip the horses as the men dropped the travois from the buckskin gelding. Working together, the tripod of poles rose high, the other poles laid into the nest and the hide cover was raised. It had been a long time since they had used the lodge, but it was familiar work and it provided a sense of home and protection for the extended family.

"I will tell Spotted Eagle you are here," declared Red Hawk as he turned to leave, "He is anxious to see you."

"And we are anxious to see him. Tell him I have something important to tell him, but if it would be better for me to come to his lodge, I will."

Red Hawk grinned, "He will come here, he has good things to tell you also." Hawk trotted off, long strides taking him down the easy slope and into the camp.

Gabe went to the stack of gear and began sorting things out, knowing much of it would be used in the tipi and lay those things aside. The saddles and other tack were bunched together at the base of a tall ponderosa that held one end of the picket line for the horses. They had already been rubbed down and had their fill of water and were now contentedly grazing on the grass, some stretching their leads to the full length to snatch up what they thought was the better grass that grew in the partial shade of the tall pines. Ezra packed several armloads of blankets and more into the tipi and the men were soon finished and sitting by the fire, anxiously waiting for the coffee to be ready.

"Ah eh!" greeted Spotted Eagle as he and Prairie Flower walked into the circle of light from the campfire.

"Hello!" answered Gabe, motioning for them to join him near the fire. There was a big grey log along one side and several flat stones on the other, evidence of this camp being used before and the visitors seated themselves on the log.

"Hawk tells me you have something important to tell?" started Eagle as he leaned forward, elbows on his knees, looking at Gabe and Ezra. As the men began to talk, Prairie Flower rose and went to where the women were busy with the meal preparation.

"We followed your trail through the south hills," said Gabe, pointing with his chin to the south, "and right after your tracks came from the mouth of the valley into the flats, another set of tracks crossed over yours." He paused, watching Eagle's reaction, then continued. "Looks to be about eighteen to twenty, no travois, came from the east mountains, continued west, but looks to me like they'll be moving north on the west edge of the basin, comin' this way."

Eagle dropped his eyes, looking at the ground between his feet and shaking his head. He looked up at Gabe and Ezra, "Blackfoot?"

Gabe nodded, glanced at Ezra who also nodded, then back to Eagle. "Cougar Woman says the same." He waited, then added, "This is a good camp, looks to be easy to defend."

"Yes, any attack would come down the valley, or around the point," he motioned to the end of the long ridge that sided the valley, the same ridge and shoulder where they now sat and pointed to the far ridge, now nothing more than a black shadow across the valley. "We have lookouts there, there and there," pointing to the far ridge, the upper valley and the point. "Our horses are on the first island. When they use up the graze, we move them to the larger island."

"Not the little one just off-shore?" asked Ezra.

"No, that is too small and the water too low, but we use it to drive the horses to the other island."

"So, if the Blackfoot were after the horses, they would have to get past the village?" asked Gabe.

"Yes, or go to the island from the point, but the water is deep there and the crossing would be hard."

"You have a large herd and it will be tempting for the Blackfoot to try to take it," suggested Gabe, but noticed a slight grin breaking on Eagle's face.

"They have tried before, many times, but have never taken our herd."

"Then I reckon you have a plan of defense to keep that from happenin'?"

The war leader of the Salish nodded, then asked, "You think they will try this night?"

"Hard tellin' Eagle, but I would think they'd want to rest up their own horses 'fore trying to take a herd that size. The Blackfoot are many things, but stupid ain't one of 'em. If they had a fight on their hands before they could get to the horses, then have to skedaddle with the herd, they wouldn't get far with tired horses and they wouldn't just leave their tired ones behind and take yours, coz that's one thing they are, is greedy!"

Eagle nodded, grinning. "I will tell our scouts and

we will be ready. I know you will be watchful, but if they do not come this night or early morning, we will speak again." He rose from the log, motioned to his woman who had been visiting with the women and playing with the little ones and they walked into the darkness, leaving Gabe and company to their meal and to settle in for the night.

6 / GROUNDWORK

It was a restless night for Gabe and company, the women fidgeted with the tired little ones and Gabe and Ezra tossed in their blankets. Gabe tossed his blankets aside and with rifle in hand, slipped from the lodge, only to be followed closely by Ezra. Gabe went to the big rock that held the coffeepot, lifted the pot and swished it around to gauge how much coffee was left and poured half in his cup and half in Ezra's. They gulped it down and walked to the edge of the trees to look over the camp below. All was quiet, nothing moved, even the dogs had gone to sleep, but Wolf stood beside the men as they looked.

Gabe turned slightly, looking at Ezra, "Spotted Eagle said they had things planned out, but I'd feel a lot better if I knew what those plans were, or at least what the Blackfoot have planned."

"So, you expect them to waltz in here and tell

you?" chuckled Ezra.

"It'd make things simpler if they did!" declared Gabe. The men were speaking in low voices, not wanting to disturb the women and the little ones, but Cougar Woman came from the tipi, searching for her man. When she saw them standing by the solitary ponderosa at the lower edge of the clearing, she walked up behind them and stood quietly. Without turning, Gabe said, "What do you think the Blackfoot will do, Cougar?"

She smiled at her man even though he hadn't looked back and answered, "They will wait until just before dark, or the next morning. It will take time for them to scout the camp and where the horses are before they decide." She looked up at the moon, that was waxing toward full, now just past a half, and added, "With the light," pointing with her chin to the moon, "I think they will try just before dark, when the village is taking their meal or later."

"Well, that would give Spotted Eagle and Plenty Bears time to get their men placed and us too," offered Ezra.

"They have been here many times; they know where to put the men and the warriors know the place well. They have done this before and have not lost the horses or captives."

"Yeah, but the Blackfoot have also done this before and might have something different planned.

Something that Eagle and Plenty Bears might not be ready for yet," surmised Gabe. "Things change and we know from our past fights that the Blackfoot can't be expected to do what you think they will."

Neither Ezra nor Cougar Woman responded to Gabe's suggestion of different possibilities, until Gabe asked, "Cougar, you were a war leader with your people. If you were leading a raid to steal horses from the Salish, what would you do?"

Cougar frowned, stepped closer to the edge of the trees and looked down on the shadowy camp below. Gabe watched as she considered, looking at the hills on the far side, the lake beyond, then turned to look at the point of the ridge that extended out into the bay. She pointed, "Eagle said he had scouts at the places they believed an enemy would strike, there, there and there," motioning to the point, the valley and the far hills. "The Blackfoot have two double hands of warriors. If I were leading, I would have one hand come from the trees, there!" pointing to the east edge of the camp below the timbered knolls. "One hand would come from here!" she turned to point at the ridge behind their camp, turning to motion them through the trees to hit the camp from the west. "One hand would come from the water!" she pointed with her chin to the sandy shore at water's edge. "The Salish would not expect an attack from the water. They would be busy at the other places where the scouts are waiting." She paused, then added, "The rest of the warriors would be at the island, gathering the horses. They would start first; the attack would only begin when the first horses hit the water. There would be much confusion, the Salish would send warriors everywhere but after the horses. They would protect their women and lodges before the horses."

Gabe was wide-eyed as he listened to Cougar, then glanced at Ezra who lifted his eyebrows and wrinkled his forehead, nodding agreement and wonder at Cougar Woman. Gabe grinned, "I'm glad I didn't have to fight against you!" he declared. She dropped her eyes and came back beside her man, slipped her arm around his waist and stood looking at the village below. Gabe glanced at Ezra, "If the Blackfoot were to do what she suggests, the Salish are in for quite a fight." He glanced at the sky, guessed the time by the position of the stars and added, "I think I'll climb up top o' this ridge, have a little look around. It'll be gettin' light 'bout the time I get there, so I might get a look at the Blackfoot or . . ." he shrugged as he turned back to the gear stacked by the big ponderosa.

Cougar followed and when Gabe stood, she said, "The Blackfoot will be near that far ridge, but will be hard to find. They could have scouts coming to this ridge to watch the village."

Gabe cocked his head to the side and asked, "Is this your way of tellin' me to be careful?"

She smiled, stepped close and slipped her arms around his waist and leaned her head back as she pulled him close, "It is my way of saying be watchful and come back to me."

Gabe bent to kiss his woman, holding her tight and as they pulled apart, "It won't matter if the entire war party is up there waitin' for me, they can't keep me from comin' back to you!"

She smiled and stepped back, letting him move past as he took to the trees to find his way to the crest of the ridge. Wolf padded beside him, then stepped out to lead the way. Cougar smiled, knowing her man would be safe with Wolf beside him.

As Gabe started up the ridge behind the camp, Ezra chose to do a walk around the perimeter of the encampment. He moved silently in the dim moonlight, his only weapon his war club at his back, choosing his route with ample cover, partly to test the scouts and partly to familiarize himself with the terrain. The men had often traveled at night and were just as comfortable moving in the moonlight as broad daylight and always moved with the silence of a catamount.

As Gabe crested the ridge, he found it to be well covered with black timber but spotted a good promontory on a rocky outcropping that held a scraggly bristlecone pine. He stepped down and sat on the ground beside the tree, letting the branches obscure him from view from anyone below. The dim light from the eastern sawtooth horizon shadowed the mountain range and slowly transformed the black night sky to the pale grey of early morn.

Gabe sat still, Wolf laying beside him, and watched the shadows lengthen with the growing light. But the darkness still lingered in the black timber of the far mountain ridge and Gabe watched as the still water of the bay that lay between the ridges caught the morning light and glistened. He smiled at the sight and knew he could use the reflected image to his advantage, until the water began to move. And it was in the reflected image that acted like a mirror to look under the wide branches of the distant trees, that gave away the location of a small morning campfire. He knew they would only use a fire if they thought it could not be seen and without the reflected image, it would be completely hidden. He grinned as he watched and it flared only for a moment, then was snuffed out, but it was enough. Now he waited.

Ezra had moved through the heavy timber that forested the valley bottom, but it was a game trail that offered silent passage. The long needles of the ponderosa and matted leaves of the winter made his passing soundless and he moved quickly across the valley floor, keeping the village off his left shoulder. He passed two tipis that were set back in the trees, but with no horses nor dogs to give away his presence, he moved quickly past. Once at the foot of the knolls, he stayed with the game trail that hugged the low shoulder and offered glimpses of the camp as well as furtive glances into the timber on the slopes above.

As he neared the point of the knolls and the lake showed through the trees, he slowed and searched for any point that would be a promontory for a scout to oversee the surrounding terrain and any movement that would betray an attack by an enemy. He stood in the shadow of a tall fir with its tangle of limbs and watched. A slight movement was the giveaway as the scout rose from his seat on the rocky outcrop. The man stood, stretched, and looked around; a bow held at his side. The beginning light of morning made the shadows mingle below and he slowly stepped back to be seated. Ezra moved closer and when close enough to strike and kill the sentry, he spoke softly in the language of the Salish, "You do not listen."

The man jumped, turning to face Ezra as he stepped into the open, revealing himself. The two recognized one another and the sentry let out his breath he did not know he was holding, "Black Buffalo! You startled me!" declared Little Badger, a friend of Red Hawk and a young man that had been to their cabin in the Big Hole basin.

Ezra nodded, stepped closer, "When you watch, you must use your eyes and your ears. In the darkness, you can hear your enemy even when you cannot see him."

"Yes, I know. It was a long journey and a long night as well. Spotted Eagle told us you and Spirit Bear had come and that you had seen Blackfoot, but he said he did not think they would come until after daylight."

"Perhaps, but what if he was wrong and the Blackfoot had started their approach before light? If I were a Blackfoot, you would be dead."

Little Badger hung his head, "I know. It will not happen again."

"Good, good," answered Ezra, then turned away, "I will go now, but be watchful, I might return!" he stated, grinning at the young man as he looked back over his shoulder, then disappeared into the shadows. He continued his walk around, moving quietly along the shore of the lake and back to the point where the west ridge pushed into the bay. He slipped from the low bank, across a broad trail and into the trees without anyone seeing nor confronting him. Once in the trees, he began his search for the scout on this end that should be overlooking the approach to the village. The obvious place for a scout was at the point of a shoulder that stood above the wide trail below and overlooked both the trail and the water between the camp and the island with the horses.

Ezra moved silently and slowly, knowing that even in the dim light, it was movement that would be the giveaway and he paused often, watching for the movement of the scout that would show his location.

He moved to a bigger ponderosa with low hanging branches, the dim light of early morning unable to penetrate the thick woods, and he dropped to one knee beside the rough barked pine, searching the shoulder for the lookout.

Without so much as a whisper, a long lance was thrust into the ground at his feet. Ezra jumped back, reaching for his war club but was stopped by a familiar voice, "It is I, Red Hawk!" Ezra leaned back, laughing and said, "That was good! I was looking for you, but I didn't know you would be the one on guard! You have learned well, Red Hawk, I will tell your father what you have done. It is not often that I have failed to hear someone near!"

"I saw you when you came from the water's edge and crossed the trail. I recognized you with your war club at your back and waited for you to come near. I moved only once, but not far and watched you as you came," he chuckled as he watched Ezra rise from under the branch of the ponderosa. They stepped into the open, looking around and laughing with one another. Red Hawk looked at Ezra, "Did Spirit Bear go to the top of the ridge to have his look?"

"You know him well. Yes, he is up there somewhere trying to find the camp of the Blackfoot." He paused, then looked at Red Hawk, "Your friend, Little Badger, did not do as well. I came up behind him and if I were a Blackfoot, he would be dead."

Red Hawk grinned, "He is learning. He has not been proven as a warrior, but he will be soon."

"If those Blackfoot come, he and others will earn their feathers or not live to see them."

"Do you believe they will come soon?"

"Hard to tell, Red Hawk, but I think we can handle anything they bring, but it might get a little bloody."

Ezra slapped the young man on the arm, turned away and started back to their camp. It would be light soon and he was yearning for some coffee to start the day right. He smiled as he thought of his family, knowing Dove would have coffee on the fire by the time he returned.

7 / REVELATION

When Gabe walked into the camp, Ezra was already enjoying his steaming coffee, holding the cup with both hands, and letting the vapors lift past his nose, savoring both the smell and the taste of his favorite brew. Although it was actually a blend of roast chicory and coffee, the men had come to appreciate the combination even more than the straight coffee. Ezra grinned at Gabe as he dropped down to the log and lay his rifle beside him, reaching for a cup to pour himself a bit of the refreshing brew.

"What'd you see?" asked Ezra, taking another sip of their diminishing supply of coffee.

"Saw where they camped and saw the two scouts they sent thisaway to check out the village," answered Gabe, between sips. "What about you? I know you didn't just sit here drinkin' coffee."

"Nope, just took a little walk around to see

what's what."

"And?" asked Gabe.

"He had the young men on point. I passed one without him seein' me and snuck up on one, Little Badger, you remember him." Ezra paused, chuckling as he remembered the boy's response, "Scared the beejeebies out of him! But I think he'll be alright now. The last one, on the point at the end of this ridge, was Red Hawk. That boy's good! He watched me long 'fore I got there and I never saw him till he stuck a lance between my feet!" He chuckled again, "we both got a laugh outta that."

"So, where do you think'll be the best place for us?"

Ezra paused, thinking, as he sipped at the strong hot brew, "I think I'd like to be down yonder, maybe cover the valley end and the far ridge. There's a good point at the end of this ridge that'll prob'ly see more action. That's where the trail from over yonder comes around the point and would be nearest the access to the island. That would be a good place for you, since you kinda like those stationary places, at least for a while."

"What about here?" asked Gabe, pointing with his chin to their camp and the ridge behind them.

"I think the women can handle this, after all, there's only 'bout twenty o' them Blackfoot, and they can't be ever'where."

The women had been across the fire working at

preparing the early meal and heard most of what was said and Cougar Woman spoke up, “Dove will be in the lodge with the little ones, I will be in the trees.”

“What if we had Red Hawk or Prairie Flower join you here?” asked Gabe.

Cougar let a smile cross her face, “Red Hawk will be where his father chooses and Prairie Flower is with child.”

Gabe frowned, glanced at Ezra and back at Cougar, “With child?”

“Yes, she told us last night and she must be careful. They lost a child before this one.”

“I see,” responded Gabe, frowning and finishing his coffee. He tossed the dregs aside and looked back at Cougar, “Then Wolf will stay with you and Dove, however you want him either with you or in the lodge with Dove.”

“He will not like that.”

“He’ll be fine. He likes you better’n me anyway and I can’t say as I blame him none,” declared Gabe, grinning at his wife and glancing down to see Wolf lift his head to look at them both. He ran his hand through the scruff of the big black’s neck and spoke softly to him, “Ain’t that right boy?” Their brief morning reverie was interrupted by the greeting from Spotted Eagle as he came into their camp.

“Greetings Spotted Eagle,” declared Gabe, motioning the war leader to be seated.

Eagle grinned at his friends, “My son tells me he got you doing a scout of our village!”

Ezra laughed, “He did! And he did a good job of it! If I had been an enemy, I would be dead at his hand!” admitted Ezra. “But did he also tell you that your other scouts would be dead at my hand?”

“He did, but you are not like most of our enemies, you are more skilled than many and my scouts would do well against most others.”

“You’re prob’ly right about that, but Little Badger is better now than he was before, just getting scared like he was will make him more careful from now on out,” observed Ezra.

“And you? Did you learn to be more careful since Red Hawk surprised you?” laughed the proud father.

“I dunno, you know how it is with us old warriors, takes a lot for us to learn anything!” responded a very somber faced Ezra, enjoying the moment of laughter with friends.

Eagle drew sober and looked at Gabe, “And what did you discover?”

Gabe scooted forward a mite, sat his coffee cup down and looked at Eagle, “Their camp is at the upper end of that far ridge and they sent two scouts out to look over your village. There is one at that end, probably looking over the point,” motioning to the north end of the ridge, “and another’n went around the south end of this ridge, prob’ly to scout the valley entrance and the south end of your village. I'd say he's prob'ly down there in the trees right now."

Spotted Eagle frowned, "Scouting us now?"

"Ummhmm, that's what I figger. And if they think your people are not fearful of an attack, they will report that you don't know they are near and they'll make a mistake."

Eagle nodded, thinking, "When do you think they will attack?"

"Where their camp is, it would be hard for them to get near your village without being seen long before they get here. So, I'm thinkin' they'll wait till dark to come close, which means they'll either come against you in the night or wait till first light. Prob'ly wait till first light."

"Yes. If they believe their scouts were not seen, they will wait until most are asleep, then come near in the night. They want the horses and to take them, they would go to the island in the dark and the moon is bright and try to move them before light." He stared at the ground, nodding his head, thinking, then looked up at Gabe, "Yes. This I will tell Plenty Bears."

Gabe scooted back on his seat and leaned back as he looked at Spotted Eagle, with a glance at Cougar Woman he asked Eagle, "Will you eat with us?"

Eagle grinned, "I must return to my lodge, Prairie Flower is preparing our meal and I must tell Plenty Bears about what we believe will happen. There are preparations that must be made."

"Well, don't go doin' too much until, oh, after mid-day, so the scouts will think there is nothing being done that would be different than any other day. Let them tell their leader it will be an easy victory," suggested Gabe, grinning, knowing that Spotted Eagle, like any war leader, would be anticipating a good fight and some degree of vengeance against their enemy, the Blackfoot. Eagle rose, nodded and hurried off to return to the village.

***

Black Snake stood before Red Crow, "They do not know we are near. There were no lookouts, no one was watching the trail, they do not expect anything."

Red Crow grunted, "You were on the ridge?"

"Yes, I could see into the village and I watched the people, but there was no one preparing weapons, or making ready for war. I moved to the point where the trail passes and there was no one. I could see the horses on the island, not the big island, but the island near to it."

Crow smiled, nodding, "Good! It will be easy to take the horses from there." He looked around at the men nearby, then back to the scout, "Did you see any guards on the island?"

"It was too far, but I could not see any."

As they spoke, a commotion at the edge of the camp told of the return of the second scout, who came to the smaller group before Red Crow. Crow glared at the man called Skunk, "You are slow returning, why?"

"I had to wait for a couple to return to the village. They came near and I could not leave without showing myself." He chuckled, "They were wooing in the bushes," and looked at Crow, saw his reproving expression and grew somber. "What I saw of the village, they are not preparing for an assault. The trail from the south would be easy to use for an attack. There is only one lodge near the trail at that end of the village and it would be easy to take without the others knowing we were near."

Crow nodded, grinning, eyes flaring in anticipation of the coming fight. He looked at the others, "We will move by the light of the moon. We will make ready to attack at first light. Weasel Horse will lead the warriors to take the island and the horses, the rest of us will move against the village in two groups." He looked at the nearby warriors, nodded toward one, "Crazy Dog will lead the warriors that will attack from the trail in the bottom, I will lead the attack around the point."

The men nodded, grinning, forcing themselves to remain quiet at a time when most would break out in war cries and screams, even dancing, but they could not allow anything to give away their presence. Crow looked at each one, "We will prepare our weapons, paint our horses and our bodies for war," lifting his voice slightly as he stood and raised his arm in the air, "and we will take many horses and more! We will shed the blood of our enemy and return to our people singing songs about our great victory!"

The men could restrain themselves no longer and many cried out in screams with their war cries, "Aiiieeee!" but were quickly silenced by the stern rebuke and stare of their leader, Red Crow. He glared at the men, motioned them away and said, "Go, make ready!"

8 / KUTENAI

White Eagle and Elk Child were belly down atop the long low ridge that extended into the waters of Salish Lake. Directly south rose Wild Horse Island and beyond that the two smaller islands until the waters lapped the south shore between two high ridges that pointed north toward where they lay atop the sparsely timbered finger ridge. Dusk was settling over the lake and White Eagle could see the glimmer of firelight from across the bay and knew that to be the village of the Salish, probably the one that Red Crow planned to attack. He glanced to his left and to the flat of the valley below them. Just back from the water was the busy camp of the Kutenai, or the Ktunaxa, as they called themselves. At the edge of the lake, several of the sturgeon nosed canoes that were common among the Ktunaxa, were grounded on the sandy shore. The camp numbered about twenty lodges, most were hide covered tipis, but several were tule mat covered tipis. The village herd of horses that White Eagle guessed to be over a hundred animals, grazed in the deep grass of the basin, above and northwest of the village.

White Eagle looked at the layout of the village and the nearby terrain, calculating, considering, planning. Elk Child, watching the horse herd, said, "It will be easy to take the horses, there are two lookouts." He paused a moment, then turned slightly to White Eagle, motioned to the herd and said, "That paint beside that black horse, looks like the one you had."

White Eagle turned to look at the animal indicated, frowned and squinted his eyes, staring at the herd in the upper end of the flats. The horse had unusual markings, a white rump, belly, and chest, with dark bay colored markings that covered all four legs, the withers, and the back, with both colors in the mane. His favorite hunter had those same markings and he was angered when it was stolen. "Yes, yes it does. It was taken when we were gone on a raid, but our people did not know if it was the Kutenai or the Crow." He stared for a moment, then turned back to the village. White Eagle nodded slowly, "We can take the village, then the horses will be ours."

"They have many warriors; two double hands of lodges mean they will have two times the number of warriors as those with us."

"We are Piikani Niitsitapi!" spat Eagle. "They are

the Ktunaxa! They are nothing!" declared an angered White Eagle. He crabbed back from the crest of the ridge and came to his feet, glaring at Elk Child, "If you are afraid, you can stay with the horses!"

"I am not afraid! I have ridden with you before and never been afraid!" Elk Child had ridden with both White Eagle and Red Crow and his loyalty was to White Eagle. Where Red Crow would send others to scout, or to take the more difficult position in an attack, White Eagle chose those things for himself. In every fight, he had always ridden at the head of his warriors and was first into the fight, but Red Crow would fall back, let the others take the brunt of the attack and then move forward, showing himself at the right time and place to take the credit for the victory. Yet White Eagle was prone to be quick tempered and often challenged his men to do more than others. Perhaps that is what made him the better of the two war leaders and the one most warriors would chose to follow.

They wended their way back to the horses, tethered in the tall pines, and mounted to return to the camp of the Blackfoot. They rode through the dark timber, crested a low saddle between two small peaks and dropped into a narrow valley that opened into a grassy flat. They were about three miles from the village of the Kutenai and his men were scattered and on their blankets beneath some tall ponderosa. When White

Eagle and Elk Child rode into the camp, the men rose and gathered around their leader.

Eagle slipped down, turned to face the men as Elk Child took the horses to the picket line and returned. Eagle began, “We will attack at first light.” He bent to the ground and grabbed a stick to draw in the dirt. “Elk Child will take Calf Shirt, Lynx Killer and those that have rifles, around the valley to the far rise to attack from there.” The Blackfoot were the first people to gain the rifle in trade from the Hudson’s Bay traders, which gave them a considerable advantage over their enemies. But they were trade fusils and lacked the accuracy of the long rifles used by the traders and trappers of the time. “I will take Stands Alone, Kicking Horse and the rest to attack from this rise. When Elk Child is ready, he will start the attack.”

“But what of the *ponokamita*?” asked Weasel Tail.

“The horses are away from the village and have two young lookouts. When the battle begins, they will run to the village and leave the horses alone. When we finish the fight, the herd will be ours!” declared White Eagle. He looked at the other warriors, saw the excitement on their faces, then ordered, “Tend to your weapons and go to your blankets. We will leave by the moonlight and be ready to attack at first light. Those with Elk Child will leave first.”

The moon was waxing to three-quarters and shone unhindered by any clouds. It was a clear night and the night sounds filled the air as Elk Child swung aboard his mount and started off toward the roundabout route to the far side of the Kutenai village. The five-mile ride would take the better part of an hour and would put them in place well before first light. Their position would be on the south edge, White Eagles' position on the north. The rising sun would bounce its brilliance off the water straight at the east edge of the village, and Eagle had factored that into his plan. They would have ample light and making their point of attack at the edge nearest the water, the sun would be off their left shoulder and their back, giving them the light and hindering the villagers. The only route of escape for the villagers would be directly into the sun, making it all the more difficult to leave.

White Eagle threw his leg over the rump of his paint gelding, sat tall with his roach headdress, and fierce in his black and white face paint that split his face at his eyes, leaving the forehead white, the lower part black, and the vermillion streaks showed as blood dripping from his eyes. His penetrating stare from deep black eyes, completed the image of impending death and fear, making his enemies stare and falter in their attack as he gave them his knife or lance. Although he had a rifle, he did not carry it into battle, preferring his bow and arrows, lance and hawk and knife. A war shield hung from the pommel of his blanket covered rawhide saddle. Eagle's chest was covered with a hair pipe bone breast plate, decorated with strips of beading, a silver band encircled his upper bicep and three feathers hung from his tall roach atop his head that waved with every move. His breech cloth was decorated with elaborate bead work that matched the design on his moccasins. Vermillion paint streaked his arms in a lightning bolt design, the same on the sides of his legs.

Eagle looked at his warriors, arrayed and painted in a similar fashion, two others with roaches, one with a buffalo horn headdress, one with the head and cape of a badger, but all had feathers and paint to make them appear even more fierce and frightening. With a simple nod, he reined his mount around to take the trail through the low saddle behind their camp and on to the long finger ridge that would be their last refuge before the battle.

White Eagle and his men tethered their mounts in the thick pines and started their approach on foot. The finger ridge pushed into the deep water of the lake, with a stretch of water behind them and the village before. Although the trees were plentiful, they were not thick, giving the men ample moonlight in the pre-dawn hour to make their way to the designated position. Once in place, Eagle motioned the men to line out toward the point, but just back from the crest of the ridge. He crawled to the crest and peered over for one last look at the village. All was quiet, nothing moved. The far side of the village had a line of trees that marked the south edge, but beyond those trees, a wide grassy flat offered no protection for the warriors with Elk Child.

White Eagle stared into the dim light, looking at the grass beyond, searching for any sign of his men approaching from the south, but he could see nothing. He glanced to his left, saw the wide line of grey silhouetting the distant mountains, and looked back at the village. The tipis were showing shadows, long shadows behind them, he noted two lodges had horses tethered close, a common practice for some men always wanting their best horse near.

Eagle frowned as he heard what sounded like distant thunder, but he quickly realized it was the sound of gunfire. But it was coming from afar, his first thought was Red Crow attacking the Salish village. He grinned but frowned as the rattling continued and grew fearful it would rouse the villagers. He squinted at the far edge of the village, saw movement, and the sudden blast of gunfire came from his warriors as they lifted their screaming war cries, charging horseback into the village from the tree line.

Eagle turned to his men, lifted his lance, and motioned them off the ridge. The ragged line charged from the low ridge, running downhill, but moving quietly, wanting to reach the village without the Kutenai knowing they were near. The first blow was struck by White Eagle, splitting the skull of a warrior as he ducked from his lodge. Eagle screamed, “Aiiieeee!” and looked for another target. He threw the flap back on the tipi, but the lodge was empty. He saw women and children running through the village, but he was concerned only with warriors. They would gather the women after the fight. He turned toward another tipi, saw a warrior drawing his bow, readying a shot at one of the attackers and Eagle threw his lance, striking the man in his chest. The throw buried the head of the lance into the bare chest, driving the warrior back as he dropped to his rear, hands on the lance shaft, then fell backwards, loosing his grip on the lance, eyes staring at the grey morning sky.

Eagle quickly retrieved his lance and turned just as he heard a screaming war cry, saw a charging Ktunaxa warrior lunging toward him with a lance. Eagle deftly stepped aside and slapped one-handed at the lance with his own, and snatched at his knife, bringing it up and into the belly of the charging warrior, ripping it up and feeling the man’s guts slide over his hand. He pushed the man away, pulled his knife back and watched the man drop to his knees, fear showing in his wide eyes, his mouth opened to speak, but he fell forward onto his own intestines that smothered his last words. Eagle stepped back, wiped his knife on the man's tunic, then slipped it into the scabbard. He reached behind him to grab his bow and nocked an arrow, took aim at a fleeing Ktunaxa warrior and let it fly. The man stumbled, the arrow flew past and the man turned back to see the shooter, just in time for the second arrow from Eagle's bow to bury itself to the fletching just below his sternum. The man, stepped back, looking down at the protruding shaft, lifted his eyes, wide with anger, to stare at White Eagle and he dropped to his knees and fell to the side in death.

Eagle nocked another arrow, looked to the far edge of the camp and saw his warriors wading and riding among the Ktunaxa, some using their rifles as clubs, others having slung their rifles at their backs, now used their tomahawks and knives as they fought in close quarters with the villagers. Eagle grinned as he saw Elk Child bury his hawk in the head of a warrior, scream his war cry and search for another. Eagle also looked everywhere for another warrior to fight. Bodies were scattered among the lodges, lying in strange contorted positions, blood pooling around the bodies. He saw two of his own men, dead or dying, lying near a tipi, outstretched in death.

Movement to his left caught his eye and he saw several canoes putting into the water. He turned and started running to the east edge of the village, nocking an arrow as he ran. He glanced to his right and saw the figure of Elk Child riding the same direction. When they came to water's edge, they saw all the canoes from the village, well out into the water, beyond bow range and all loaded with women and children, frantically paddling to make their escape. Eagle turned to Elk Child, "They will have to come ashore somewhere, have one of the men watch. We will finish off the Ktunaxa, then take the horses."

Elk Child saw one of their men, bloody from the battle but with none of his own blood and motioned him over. It was Kicking Horse, a good man and proven warrior. Elk Child pointed at the retreating canoes, "Watch, see where they go ashore. We will finish the village, take the horses. You come as soon as they land." Kicking Horse nodded, looked around and finding a sizeable rock, took a seat and started his vigil.

9 / SALISH

The three-quarter moon was lowering in the western sky but the trees atop the long ridge held their nighttime shadows close. Before the first light, the long shadow of the ridge would lay across the camp, darkening the valley and aiding the defenders as they began to move to their designated defense. Gabe and Ezra had ridden to the top of the ridge, tethered their horses and sat beside the bristlecone pine to watch the moonlit valley below. For the Blackfoot to make an attack, they had to cross the wide flat and nothing had moved yet.

Gabe glanced at the moon, looked at the valley below, "They gotta be movin' soon, if they're gonna."

"Ummhmm, how 'bout now?!" declared Ezra as he pointed to the tree line that pointed furthermost into the valley. It first appeared as if the trees were moving, the band was so close to one another, then they separated. One bunch, about six or seven started across the flats in a diagonal line toward the south end of the big ridge, another bunch of similar size, split off and moved around the broad base of the low ridge, appearing to follow the edge of the lake toward the crossing to the island. The remainder took a direct course toward the trail that would lead around the point to the village.

Gabe looked at Ezra, back at the band of attackers, "Looks like we got it to do!"

"Yup!" answered Ezra as he stood and started back to the tethered mounts. As Gabe walked beside him, he said, "Keep your topknot on!"

"You do the same." They swung aboard their mounts and started off in different directions, Ezra to the south end of the ridge and the mouth of the valley, Gabe to the point and the narrow trail. As they rode, both men were visualizing what they would do, knowing they had to do their part, but the Salish warriors would be in the fore of the fight, at least that was the plan.

Ezra kept his Lancaster rifle in the scabbard under his right leg, the war club, the iron wood club with the halberd blade and spike and inlaid stone, was Ezra's preferred weapon and it hung from a lanyard behind his back. He unconsciously touched his metal bladed tomahawk, his over/under pistol at his belt and his knife in its sheath. He breathed deep, readying his nerves and his determination, he was fighting for his family and his friends and would not be deterred. His nostrils flared as he flexed his muscles that shone in the moonlight with the thin layer of bear grease, he was bare headed with two feathers tucked into his hair at the nape of his neck. Dove had beaded a fringed band of buckskin that was wrapped around his upper bicep. His fringed buckskin breeches flittered in the breeze of his movement, his moccasined feet were tucked into the stirrups and his eyes flared with the rising sense of the impending battle.

He reined up in the trees at his chosen point, to await the attackers. He would follow their lead, if they chose to stay mounted, he would follow aboard his battle proven bay gelding, but if they picketed the animals and made their approach on foot, he would follow on foot. The plan was to drive them into the waiting warriors led by Running Wolf, warriors that were stationed at the southern edge of the camp. Ezra would take them from behind and start the battle with his first shot.

His wait was brief and the Blackfoot warriors continued toward the camp, single file, following the trail. Ezra waited for the last warrior to pass, but after five passed, there were no more. Ezra frowned, realizing the other two must have taken a trail over the ridge, which meant they might encounter Cougar and Dove. But he had to follow the others toward the camp and he turned his bay to work his way through the woods, parallel with the trail and behind the Blackfoot. The big bay picked his steps carefully, keeping to the thick layer of ponderosa needles and matted aspen leaves. The attackers were nearing the first tipi that was set back in the trees, and Ezra watched as they moved to make a line across the valley, preparing to attack.

Ezra slipped his rifle from the scabbard, eared back the hammer as quietly as possible, and brought the muzzle up to take aim. His bay had been shot from many times and Ezra always warned him by rubbing the barrel of the rifle on his neck as he brought it up. The bay turned his head back to see his rider, then lowered his head as if to cover or shield his ears. Ezra watched, saw the other warriors down the line looking toward the second man from the end and he waited. The man slowly lifted his arm and as he brought it high, Ezra touched off the Lancaster that bucked, roared, and spat smoke and lead. Ezra leaned slightly to the side, saw the man tumble from his horse, heard the scream of one of the other warriors and saw them start their charge. Ezra slipped the rifle into the scabbard and brought his war club around while he dug heels into the ribs of the bay and lunged forward in pursuit of the nearest Blackfoot.

Gabe slipped from his saddle, loosely tethered Ebony in the trees and checked his weapons. He sat down and strung the Mongol Bow, hung the quiver of arrows at his hip, slipped the Ferguson rifle from the scabbard and checked the priming and quietly snapped the frizzen down. He put the two over/under saddle pistols in his belt with the swivel barrel Bailes pistol. Touched his tomahawk, felt his knives hanging at his back and started through the trees. He knew where Red Hawk waited and silently moved up behind him. He whispered, "Behind you," to let the young warrior know he was near, and as Red Hawk turned he added, "They're coming. Seven by the lake, prob'ly goin' to the island after the horses, and seven more coming along the trail."

Red Hawk had chosen a point of rock that overlooked the trail and was near enough to shoot from with his bow. Below the point was a thicket of scrub oak and a few chokecherry bushes, a couple small juniper and more rocks. On the far side of the trail, the bank dropped off toward the water, but held more scrub oak brush. Gabe looked it over, knew where the Blackfoot would approach and shook his head. He remembered other times when he faced a number of attackers out to do harm to his family or friends and time and again, he lay in wait to ambush them and turn the tide of the battle. But an ambush just did not sit well with Gabe, his way had always been as his father advised and face the trouble head on, man to man. Even when the numbers were against him and now he was faced with another situation that seemed to demand he lay in wait and ambush the band that outnumbered him. But he shook his head, *Not again, I'm not going to lie in wait and take them by surprise. I'd rather stand face to face and look my enemy in the face so he can see who he is to do battle with and I can see them. Anyone can shoot from cover, or hiding, but as my father often said, 'Stand up to your enemy. Let them see who they come against!'* He took a deep breath, let it out, looked at Red Hawk and whispered, "Follow me."

Spotted Eagle led his men onto the island shortly after dark. They were situated around the perimeter that faced the crossing where any assault would have to approach and now waited for the signal from shore that the Blackfoot were approaching. Eagle and Gabe, or Spirit Bear as he was known among the Salish, had agreed on the call of the nighthawk to give the warning the Blackfoot were approaching. The word was passed among the eight other warriors and all waited for the night cry. With the sounds of the lapping waves against the shore, the usual sounds of the night with owls, frogs, cicadas, and more, the men had been lulled into a snooze. But when the repeated cry of the nighthawk with its shrill peent, peent, followed by a deep throated boom like the hoot of an owl, every warrior was instantly awake, staring at the shore for shadows to show against the light sand and stones at water's edge.

Gabe had given the signal of the nighthawk, then stepped to the middle of the trail, nocking an arrow and taking a spread-legged stance. His rifle hung from a sling at his back. He glanced at Red Hawk who stood at his left, partially shielded by the brush, but standing ready, his lance at his back and an arrow nocked as he held the bow at his side.

Red Hawk looked at the tall white man, his dark blonde hair hanging to his shoulders, his whiskered face showing rough but split with his grin that showed white teeth in the last of the moonlight. His eyes flashed in the darkness, his buckskin tunic with beads over each shoulder accented his broad shoulders. The grey light in the eastern sky was at his back and the fearsome features of the tall man would be made all the more mysterious as his shadow stretched out before him.

Ezra slapped legs to the big bay and set off after the nearest warrior. The Blackfoot saw the man coming and kicked his animal to try to get away, but Ezra had the jump on him and quickly came near. The warrior turned, wide-eyed, and tried to twist around to meet the charge, but Ezra had purposely moved to the right side, the off side for a bow wielding attacker, and with a wide swing over his head, the war club struck the man on the side of his head, splitting it open and knocking him from his mount. Without hesitating, Ezra looked for the next man, saw him charging after a fleeing woman and screamed his own war cry! The Blackfoot looked up to see the massive black man charging, screaming, and swinging a big club. He ducked to avoid the swing, but Ezra dropped the head of the war club, driving the blade into the warrior's back between his shoulder blades. The force of the blow split open the Blackfoot's torso, blood shooting out, as Ezra jerked the blade free. He turned away, saw the nearest Blackfoot, readying a shot with his bow and arrow, but Ezra slapped legs to the bay, driving him into the Blackfoot's horse, ruining the shot as the arrow fluttered high. The man reached for another arrow, then heard the whistle of the war club, looked up and met the club with his face. Ezra had turned the head to hit the man with the flat of the club, but the force of the blow was not hindered and the man's forehead caved in the with heavy ironwood knot.

He started for his next target but saw three arrows strike the chest of the man almost simultaneously and Ezra turned to see a grinning Running Wolf and Little Badger, standing side by side with another warrior. Ezra turned to search for another, saw a riderless horse and looked back to see two warriors take down another attacker, one with a lance, the other with his tomahawk. But there were no other attackers. Several Salish warriors were also looking for others, ready with arrows nocked on their bows, or standing ready with a lance, but there were no others to fight.

Ezra motioned toward the front of the village, turned to Running Wolf, "Let some of your men go to the trail, they might be needed. But leave some here also!"

Running Wolf nodded and began barking orders to the remaining warriors. Ezra gigged the bay forward as he started through the camp, looking for any Blackfoot, moving closer to the point where he expected to find Gabe and Red Hawk.

The shuffling of hooves of walking horses, muffled by the thick shrubbery, came from around the wide bend. There were no heavy leather saddles like the white man used that would creak with the movement of the horses, no metal weapons or tack that would rattle to give them away, but the huff and snort of a horse, the shuffle of their walk, were obvious sounds of their approach. Within moments, the first of the riders appeared and did not hesitate, until the first rider saw the figure in the trail. He reined up and leaned forward, shielding his eyes from the dim light of early morn that was behind the figure and he whispered to the warrior beside him. At the same time, the reverberating sound of a rifle shot came from beyond the point and all knew the battle was on. The others crowded behind, pushing the horses a step or two more, anxious to get in the fight, until the deep voice came from the shadow, speaking the tongue of the Piikani Blackfoot.

"I am Spirit Bear! I am a friend to the great Salish people! I will kill any one and every one that dares to come near!"

The Blackfoot spoke to one another, several laughing and pointing because the distance was greater than a bow could shoot, until the shadowy figure lifted his bow and let an arrow fly. The feathered shaft whispered across the one hundred yards between them and buried itself in the chest of the man in the lead, the warrior known as Black Snake, chosen by Red Crow to take the lead as Crow rode behind him. The arrow penetrated the body, the point and shaft protruding out his back, the feathers fluttering at his chest. The man had been knocked backwards and tumbled over the rump of his horse to fall in a heap at the foot of the horse ridden by Red Crow.

Several of the warriors shouted, "Aiiieeee," and screamed their war cries as they slapped legs to the horses to lunge forward, charging the man in the trail. One warrior fired his rifle and Gabe heard the bullet whistle past, but he continued his fight. Another arrow from the Mongol bow took a warrior in the neck, driving him off his horse, but the animal kept going. The third arrow also took a warrior in the sternum, lifting him from his mount and dropping him in a seated position, only to be trampled by the horse and warrior behind.

Gabe let the bow fall at his side, kept there by a tether around his shoulder and lifted his rifle, earing back the hammer as he lifted and shot from the hip. The bullet grazed the neck of a horse and flipped the rider end over end to land splayed out on his face, to be trampled. Gabe dropped his rifle, pulled the two saddle pistols, cocking the hammers as he lifted them. He extended his arms, drew a quick aim, and dropped the hammers. Both pistols bucked, roared, and spat smoke, startling the nearest horses, both riderless, to take to the brush beside the trail. Gabe saw one bullet strike, but the second missed, making the warrior duck away, yet as he bent toward his horse's neck, Gabe saw an arrow take the man in the chest and he knew Red Hawk had shown himself. Gabe cocked the second hammers and fired at the two remaining warriors, one taking the blast full on in his face and exploding out the back of his head, the other apparently hit in the shoulder, causing him to drop to the neck of his mount and pull it around. Before Gabe could snatch up his belt pistol, the warrior, Red Crow, was lying low on the neck of his horse and disappeared around the bend of the trail, leaving nothing but the dead bodies of his warriors and a dust cloud behind.

Gabe frowned as he heard rifle fire, but it was coming from far across the bay and beyond the islands.

He shook his head, wondering if there were more Blackfoot, but intent on the battle they were waging here. In the growing light of early morning, he looked to the edge of the island and saw some activity, but not what he expected.

Spotted Eagle had instructed his men well, they waited in total silence as they listened to the splashing of water as the Blackfoot approached the island, swimming through the cold water. The Blackfoot had chosen to leave their horses ashore, believing they could catch the horses on the island and ride one off as they herded the others. All would have to swim, but the attack had to be quiet in case there were more warriors than expected.

As the first few came from the water, nothing happened until they gathered closer, one man giving the instructions about rounding up the horses. As they turned, a hail of arrows whispered through the air and took down four of the attackers, wounded two more and before they could take cover, more arrows found their mark and the Salish charged. But only one Blackfoot remained, holding the arrow imbedded in his arm, and was still alive. He grabbed for his knife, but a tomahawk split his skull and he crumbled to the ground amid the shouts and war cries of the jubilant Salish.

10 / TOGETHER

Silence draped over the valley and the village of the Salish. No war cries, no screams of triumph, for a few moments each one paused, absorbing the gravity of the events and what could have happened. Yet realizing they were spared, the enemy vanquished, silence was chased away on the skirts of shouts of rejoicing and the work that must be done. The warriors were already stripping the downed enemy of anything of value and usefulness. The bodies had to be taken away and buried and the bodies of their own had to be tended.

Gabe and Red Hawk stood silently for a moment until the restlessness of the enemies' horses below the trail caught their attention. Gabe looked at the island, saw Spotted Eagle leading his warriors in the task of disposing of the bodies of the Blackfoot and knew they would soon come ashore. He glanced around to see the horses of the dead were snatching mouthfuls of grass along the trail and he spoke to Red Hawk, "If you catch up those horses, I'll start draggin' them," nodding to the bodies, "over to that edge of the trail and dumpin' 'em over. We can probably cave in that bank enough to cover 'em."

"But the weapons and plunder?" asked Red Hawk, anxious to take his trophies.

"I'll pile it all in a bunch and you can have your pick. I don't think they'll have anything I want."

Red Hawk looked askance at the tall man, wonder showing in his eyes, "But you killed so many. I have never known of anyone to do what you did. In all that, I sent one arrow and you took down five! You never moved!"

"Hawk, each time you find yourself facing an enemy, you must do what you can and all you can. Don't stop and think about it, the numbers you face, the size of your enemy, anything. Just do what you can." Gabe paused, dropped his eyes, and walked to the side to lay down his rifle. He sat down, reloaded all his weapons, then stood and started at his task. He had stripped each one, stacked the weapons and plunder at the side, then dragged four of the bodies to the edge of the trail, when Red Hawk reached for the next one. Gabe paused, looked at the young man, then glanced to the edge of the island, "Looks like Spotted Eagle and the others are coming, so, I'm gonna go check on Cougar

Woman and Ezra. You do with that what you will," nodding to the pile of plunder. Red Hawk nodded as he glanced at the pile of weapons that included two rifles and more, and the grin of youth split his face, knowing that the horses and the plunder would make him a wealthy young man and the envy of others.

Gabe grabbed his rifle and bow then went to the trees to fetch Ebony. He slipped the rifle into the scabbard, unstrung the bow and slipped it into its case, hung the quiver at the edge of the cantle and swung aboard. He was tired, but relieved that it was over, at least for now and was anxious to get back to his family.

He was pleased to see Cougar Woman seated on the log, talking with Ezra and Dove while the little ones lay nearby on the buffalo robes. She looked up as he came near, then stood to greet him and help him strip Ebony and tether the big black before returning to the circle. They sat together on the log and Gabe asked, "Alright, tell me."

Cougar frowned, "Tell you? Tell you what?"

He chuckled and said, "What happened while we were gone. I can tell by the way you're looking and acting that you didn't just sit around doin' nothin'!"

She grinned, glanced at Dove and Ezra and answered, "There were two that came near. I took one from behind, she," nodding to Dove, "shot one as he came into camp." She looked at her man with raised eyebrows and a somber expression like what had happened was a common event and nothing unusual.

Ezra grinned, "I'll tell ya 'bout it later. There was a little more to it than that, but you know how they," nodding toward the women, "don't like talkin' 'bout stuff like that. Now, if it was a question about the young'uns, they'd blather on all day, but you know, something like a life and death struggle, well, that's nothing."

Gabe shook his head, glanced at his woman and then to Dove, then reached for a cup to pour himself some coffee. He sat back to sip the brew when a disturbance from below the trees caused him to turn to see Red Hawk walking into their camp. He looked from one to the other, "My father asks that you come below. There is something for you to see."

"Oh, and what might that be?" asked Gabe, unwilling to surrender his seat and his coffee.

"It is not for me to say, but it is important," replied the young man, his expression solemn.

"Just me?"

"No, all of you."

"Hmmm, sounds a little ominous," he looked from one to another, then nodded as he rose. The women put the little ones in the cradle boards and Cougar lifted Bobcat to Gabe as Ezra took the hand of Chipmunk and the two families started after Red Hawk to go to the village. The village appeared to be abandoned, but they soon saw the people gathered at the shore of the lake, standing close and facing the water.

One of the women saw Gabe and company nearing and spoke to Plenty Bears who motioned for the people to step aside and let them through. As they moved through the crowd and came near Plenty Bears, they saw what the commotion was all about. Grounded at the shore were several sturgeon nose canoes, and at water's edge stood many women and children, speaking to Spotted Eagle and others. Eagle turned to see Gabe and motioned him and Cougar close. As they neared, Spotted Eagle said, "These are Kutenai. They were attacked this morning the same time we were attacked. The women escaped in the canoes, but they believe their village has been destroyed and their men killed."

One of the women started speaking rapidly, pleading with Eagle and anyone else, but Eagle shook his head and turned back to Gabe and Cougar. "Their language is different. I do not know it. We have used signs, but . . ." he shrugged, looked at Cougar. "Perhaps if you would try?"

Cougar nodded and stepped close, she began, using sign as she spoke and the woman was relieved that someone could understand them. After they spoke for a short while, Cougar nodded and turned back to Gabe and Spotted Eagle. "She is certain all of the men were killed, and the village destroyed. They saw the smoke from the water. She said there were more than three double hands of warriors, young and old, and six double hands of horses. They have nothing, they had no time to gather their things and now they are afraid to return to their village." She paused, looked at Eagle and added, "I told her that they would find help and shelter here among the Salish." She looked to Gabe, "I also told her we would try to find the Blackfoot and get the horses back, for the horses are all they have to provide for themselves."

Spotted Eagle looked from Cougar Woman to Gabe and then to his chief, Plenty Bears. The chief stepped forward, lifted his hands to speak to the people, "We will help our friends of the Ktunaxa. All our people must take some to their lodges with them to feed and shelter them. We," nodding to his Shaman and War Leader, implying the council of elders, "will meet to decide what must be done."

Cougar turned, signed, and spoke to the woman that had been their spokesman, then motioned for her and hers to follow. Gabe lifted his eyebrows in surprise as the woman, with a touch of grey in her hair, was followed by two quite attractive girls, obviously twins and about fifteen summers, who obediently followed, eyes down as they walked past the gathered people. Dove motioned to another woman who held a child at her hip with another standing, clinging to her dress. The woman nodded and followed Dove. Gabe and Ezra watched, looked at each other and shrugged and started following the group back to their camp.

Ezra glanced at Gabe, “Guess we’ll be goin’ huntin’ soon.”

“Ummhmm, gonna be needin’ some meat for certain,” answered Gabe.

Gabe and Ezra purposefully bided their time as they sauntered toward the camp, allowing the women time to get the visitors settled. As the men walked into their camp, it was already as if the extended family had been together for some time. The girls had taken to the little ones and now sat with them on the buffalo robes, Chipmunk and the girl that had clung to her mother’s dress, were sitting together playing with a drum/rattle of Chipmunk’s, and the women were working together to prepare the mid-day meal. Gabe glanced at Ezra and gave a slight nod toward the coffee pot that danced near the fire and the men sat down on the long grey log, reaching for their cups. All the women looked at them and the two visitors spoke to Cougar, obviously asking questions about the strange men that were their husbands. Ezra grinned at Gabe, “Bet their asking about a white man and a black man havin’ Shoshone women for wives!”

Gabe chuckled, “Well, we ain’t exactly what they’d expect to find in a Salish camp, but they’re probably just talkin’ ‘bout our whiskers. They ain’t used to men havin’ whiskers.”

Ezra chuckled, “Yeah, I’m sure that’s it.”

11 / PIIKANI

White Eagle and Elk Child rode in the lead, the horse herd following and driven by the remainder of the band. It had been a successful raid on the Kutenai, although the women and children escaped, White Eagle's band had taken the horse herd, many scalps, and much plunder from the village before they left it in flames. At a shout from behind them, Elk Child turned to see three riders coming at a canter around the herd, one with his lance lifted high to get their attention. "Someone is coming," stated Child, speaking to White Eagle. Both men reined up, causing the horse herd to slow and the horses to snatch mouthfuls of grass as they lingered.

"It is Red Crow!" came the cry from Calf Shirt who rode beside Red Crow. Kicking Horse was on the other side as they escorted him as if he were an enemy. As they rode near, White Eagle lifted his hand for them to stop as he frowned at Red Crow and looked behind him for the rest of his raiding party. He glared at Crow, "Why are you here?"

"The Salish and one known as Spirit Bear have killed them all!" he waved his arm behind him, glowering at White Eagle.

White Eagle frowned, "All of your men were killed? And yet you live? How can it be so?"

Crow nudged his mount closer, coming alongside White Eagle, the motion prompted the others to ride on as the herd began to move again. Crow looked at White Eagle, "We made a plan. Weasel Horse and Skunk and others went to the island for the horses, Crazy Dog and one hand of warriors attacked the village from the high end of the valley, Black Snake, me, and one hand of warriors took the trail around the point to attack. But they knew we were coming and waited. A white man, Spirit Bear, was one of many that stopped us on the trail and killed all those with me! I was wounded," he bent forward and showed the blood at his shoulder, then looked back at White Eagle. "Before I was hit, I killed three Salish! But I was hit, fell to the neck of my horse, lost my weapon and the horse spooked. He was away from the camp when I was able to stop him!"

"You said the others were all killed, how do you know this?" asked a stern White Eagle.

"I rode back, but there were no more sounds of

battle and I took to the trees. I was high up on the ridge and saw them scalping the bodies and more."

White Eagle glared at Red Crow, "You should have known the Salish and the island of horses has never been taken. To take a raiding party against the big village was foolish!"

"You attacked a village!" he retorted.

"A Kutenai village! They are not the warriors like the Salish! The village was not as large and the horses were near. We did not have to split our numbers like you did!" spat White Eagle, his contempt for his rival evident.

"And now you flee?" chided Red Crow.

"We go to take another Kutenai village!" snarled White Eagle. "If you come, you will not lead and you will do as I say!" demanded White Eagle.

Red Crow started to protest, but stopped himself, knowing he had little choice. If he were to return to their people without his warriors, he would be exiled in shame. But if he stayed with White Eagle's band, he could gain some horses and plunder and return to the village as the warrior he believed himself to be and he would still be a war leader. And perhaps he could redeem himself in the next raid on the Kutenai.

***

Spotted Eagle and Red Hawk came into the camp of Gabe and company, exchanging greetings as they were seated beside the fire ring. Off to the side stood a rack with fresh cut strips of venison from a deer taken by Ezra in the early afternoon, smoke curling up from the coals and alder branches. A haunch of the venison hung from a high branch, cooling and curing in the shade of the ponderosa. Gabe offered Eagle and Hawk a cup of coffee, and both declined, Eagle squirming a little on his seat, glancing from the smoldering coals to Gabe. With a low chuckle, Gabe said, "Whatever it is, you can speak freely Spotted Eagle."

Eagle looked from Gabe to the group of women that were cutting up more of the venison and talking. Gabe noticed Red Hawk casting a furtive glance toward the twins that were tending the little ones as they squirmed on the buffalo robe, a glance that was returned with a smile from one of the girls. Eagle cleared his throat and began, "The council met and talked of the Kutenai and the Blackfoot. It was suggested that I go to the site of the village and see what has been done, report back to the council. I would have you join me."

"Just the two of us?" asked Gabe.

"If it is as the women say, the Blackfoot will be gone. We are to see what is left to be done and where the Blackfoot have gone."

"Sounds reasonable. What about the horses?"

"The council was not concerned about the horses. If we were to go after the Blackfoot, it would leave our village open for attack. We do not know how many raiding parties of the Blackfoot are about. I did not expect more than what attacked our village and to know another band hit the Ktunaxa, we do not know how many or if that is the only other raiding party."

Gabe nodded, glanced at Ezra who gave a slight nod of understanding also, then looked back at Spotted Eagle. "In the morning?"

"Yes. First light."

Gabe nodded, reached for the coffee, and poured himself a cup, again offered some to Spotted Eagle who rose to leave. Red Hawk was still seated, and Gabe offered him a cup which he accepted, with a glance toward the girls. Spotted Eagle looked at his son, let a slight grin tug at the corner of his mouth as he glanced to Gabe, then turned to leave. With a wave of his hand over his shoulder, he walked through the thin line of trees and took the trail to the camp below.

Gabe looked at Red Hawk, "So, you get all those horses and plunder sorted out?"

"Yes. I have my own lodge now. I traded two horses for the lodge of Buffalo Tail. He was killed and his woman, White Fox, returned to her family. She was glad to have the horses and I have plenty," replied Hawk, again glancing to the twins.

Gabe grinned, and said, "You have done well. Will

you eat with us?" He knew what the answer would be from the young man who appeared to be more than a little interested in the girls, and when Red Hawk smiled and nodded, he lifted his voice to Cougar Woman, "Cougar, Red Hawk is going to eat with us."

She looked at her husband with a bit of a frown, not understanding why he would make such an obvious statement, but when his eyes went to Red Hawk and then to the girls, she understood, smiled, and nodded. "It is good. Red Hawk is always welcome at our fire." The women quickly finished the cutting of the meat and Dove brought several steaks to the fire ring. Under her arm she had several willow withes that would be used to hang the steaks over the fire, leaving room for the pot of vegetables and the dutch oven with biscuits. The men stepped back from the fire and went to the stack of gear, getting well out of the way of the women and sat on the rocks to sip their coffee.

Ezra looked at Red Hawk, "So, now that you have your own lodge, you thinkin' 'bout gettin' yourself a woman?"

Although Red Hawk was certain the twins did not know the tongue of the Salish, he glanced their direction and dropped his gaze between his feet as he mumbled, "I have been thinking of that, yes." He fidgeted a little before he forced himself to look up at Gabe and Ezra, purposefully not looking in the direction of the girls. Both men were grinning as Gabe said,

"Looks to me like you're gonna have to practice your sign language if you expect to go courtin'."

Red Hawk frowned as he looked from Gabe to Ezra, and asked, "What is courtin'?"

Both men chuckled and Ezra nodded to Gabe to explain. Gabe squirmed as he sat on his rock, then seated himself on the ground and began, "Well, it's like this. Different peoples have different ways of a man and a woman getting together, you know, to become man and wife." He paused, looking at Red Hawk for a glimmer of understanding, and continued. "See, with the Shoshone, it's just getting to know one another, sneakin' off alone and such, and if you like each other, then the man has to go to the father and get permission and give gifts."

Red Hawk smiled, nodded, "That would be easy."

"Well, sort of, but I understand it's different among the Salish and prob'ly different with the Kutenai, or Ktunaxa."

"Yes, among my people, the man tells his mother, and she talks to the mother of the woman. If they agree, then the mother of the man and her family make a blanket which the man uses to go to the woman and . . ." he grinned, "I do not know what they do with the blanket."

"I take it you are interested in one of the twins?" asked Ezra.

"They are beautiful! Yes, I would like to think of

one of them for a wife, but what do I do?"

Gabe grinned, trying to maintain a serious composure, then said, "How 'bout we talk to our women and they can find out from the mothers," pointing his chin in the direction of the four women working at the fire, "and then we'll know what to do."

"You don't think you're kinda rushin' things?" asked Ezra. "After all, you just met 'em today!"

"Why? Does it take a long time to know these things?" asked Red Hawk, his brow furrowing in concern.

Gabe and Ezra glanced at one another, grinning and chuckling, as Ezra answered, "Not always."

"And there are others among the warriors that have seen the twins. I cannot risk losing them to another warrior."

"Them?" asked Gabe, frowning.

Red Hawk frowned, realizing what he said, "*One* of them."

12 / WOMEN

Among the plains Indians, many tribes, such as the Blackfoot, Shoshone, and Crow, speak a unique dialect of the Algonquian language, making their language their own. Other tribes, like the Salish, Kutenai, Nez Percé, and more, have a totally unique language. Because Cougar Woman had traveled with her father as a trader, she had become versed in many languages, but was not fluent in the languages that were not of the Algonquian origins. She did have a working knowledge of the Kutenai and had learned both the Salish and Blackfoot and become fluent in them. But women have a way of communicating that often baffles men and the women around the fire of Cougar Woman and Grey Dove, appeared to have little difficulty talking.

As the men talked together apart from the fire, Gabe noticed the women often glancing their way, mostly smiling, and laughing, and he knew they were the subject of the women's discussion. He also assumed, much of the talk was centered on Red Hawk and his obvious interest in the twins. But Gabe knew better than to question the ways of women, especially when they outnumbered the men, two to one. When Cougar called, "The food is ready!" the men rose and walked to the fire, anxious to partake of the food they had been smelling for some time.

As the men were seated, the women dished up the food into the wood trenchers and handed it off to the men, Cougar to Gabe, Dove to Ezra, and one of the girls, Running Fox, passing the trencher to Red Hawk, smiling broadly as their hands touched. Fox dropped her eyes and stepped back to stand beside her sister, Little Rabbit. Red Hawk sat back, keeping his eyes on the twins until they turned away and he dropped his eyes to the food. Once the men had theirs, the women dished up their own portions, using the remaining wooden trenchers and some tin plates from the packs.

Cougar sat beside Gabe and spoke softly to him, "I asked the mother of the girls about the way of the Ktunaxa and taking a mate. She was not surprised; she saw Red Hawk looking at her girls."

"So, what does he have to do?" asked Gabe.

"Their way is similar to the Salish. The mothers speak, and a blanket is made. But they also use a flute, like the Sioux people."

"Would she speak with the mother of Red Hawk?"

"After what happened with their men, she is concerned for her girls. I think she will listen."

Gabe glanced at Red Hawk, gave a slight nod, and saw a broad smile split Red Hawk's face as he glanced toward the girls. Red Hawk quickly finished his meal and came close to Gabe and Cougar Woman and went to one knee behind them. "There are many here for your lodge. I have an empty lodge and some of these could use it if they chose."

Cougar grinned as she looked sideways at Gabe, then turned back with a sober face to look at Red Hawk, "That is kind of you Red Hawk. I will speak to Basket Woman and see if she would like to take her little ones to your lodge."

Red Hawk frowned, "Little ones?" he asked, looking around at the Ktunaxa.

Gabe and Cougar laughed, then Cougar said, "Perhaps it would be better if I spoke to Stands Tall and her girls, Running Fox and Little Rabbit."

Red Hawk dropped his head, shaking it side to side and lifted his eyes to look at Cougar Woman, "I should have known your ways. You were like that with Two Drums and Little Owl when we were at your cabin. But perhaps it would be good for both families to use the lodge." He chuckled and stood, looked at the girls who had returned to the buffalo robe with the little ones and sat talking to one another, glancing occasionally in the direction of the others and Red Hawk.

He stepped back into the shadows as Cougar spoke to Stands Tall to tell of the unused lodge. When the mother asked about Red Hawk, Cougar turned back to look at him, "Will you stay in the lodge?"

Red Hawk frowned, "No, I will return to the lodge of my father."

Cougar told Stands Tall and the woman smiled and nodded, then spoke to the girls who smiled, looked up at Red Hawk and answered their mother. It appeared that everyone was in agreement and Red Hawk said, "I will go to make ready and speak to my father's woman as well. I will return to show them the way to the lodge." Cougar knew what Hawk would be telling his mother and smiled as she watched him leave.

When Red Hawk approached the cookfire where his father, Spotted Eagle and his woman, Prairie Flower, were seated and having their meal, they looked up, surprised, and Eagle said, "I thought you would be with Spirit Bear and the others."

"I was, but I have offered my lodge to the women of the Kutenai and I have come to prepare it," explained Red Hawk, squatting on his haunches beside the fire.

"Does that mean you will be with us this night?" asked Spotted Eagle.

"If that is agreeable with you."

Spotted Eagle looked to his woman, who smiled and nodded, then back to his son. "Is there something else?"

Red Hawk looked from his father to Prairie Flower, "It is the custom with the Ktunaxa when a man wants a woman for his own, he is to speak with his own mother first then she must speak to the mother of the woman." He paused, remembering his own mother, Whispering Wind, who was killed in a Blackfoot raid, and looked up at Prairie Flower, his father's new wife.

Prairie Flower looked at Spotted Eagle, "It is as you said. He has seen a woman he wants for his own, but is it acceptable for him to take a woman of the Ktunaxa?"

"The Kutenai, or Ktunaxa, have been allies and it is not uncommon for the bands to take a woman from another band. If they were enemies, and the girl had been taken as a captive, it would also be allowed," explained Spotted Eagle.

"And do you like this union?" asked Flower.

He showed a somber expression as if in deep thought, then looked sternly at his son, "Are you ready to take a woman for your own?"

"Yes, I have proven myself as a warrior and hunter, it is time I have a woman as my wife."

"Do you know that you will have to take her mother and her sister into your lodge and provide for them until they have their own man."

Red Hawk frowned, realizing he had not considered the possibility of having to provide for the family, but the thought of either of the girls being his woman was enough to allay any concerns of the others. He breathed deep, lifting his shoulders, and sitting more erect, "Yes, I understand that and I believe I am ready for this."

Flower asked, "Then according to their way, I am to talk to the mother?"

"Yes, and according to the way of our people, there must also be a blanket." He paused a moment, looked at his father, "And they said it was also the custom for the man to use a flute to play before the lodge." He frowned as he thought of it, then looked to his father for an explanation.

"I have heard of this. Our Shaman, Raven's Wing, would know of this and could show you about the flute." He glanced at Flower, looked at the dim light of dusk, then suggested, "If you will, you could talk to the mother while we go to see Raven's Wing." Flower nodded, lifting her eyebrows in surprise and prepared to go to the camp of Cougar Woman and the others to talk with the mother of the girls.

When Prairie Flower came into the circle of light, she was warmly greeted by Cougar Woman and Grey Dove, who introduced her to the two women of the Kutenai. When it was explained that she was the wife of Spotted Eagle and had come to speak to Stands

Tall, the other women smiled and nodded, moving away to allow the women room to talk in private. But Stands Tall asked Cougar to assist in the conversation, making it easier for both to understand. As the three women spoke, there was laughing and chattering, moments of reminiscing, but the rest of the time was spent in making preliminary plans. The courtship would be the first for both mothers and with the two cultures, it would be special for all concerned. As the conversation lulled, Stands Tall asked, "Which of my girls is he wanting?"

Prairie Flower looked at Cougar, who shrugged, and looked back at Stands Tall, "I do not know. But he has said he is willing for all of you to be a part of his lodge. He knows he will be responsible to take care of all of you."

Stands Tall grew somber, and stated, "It is not unusual for our people to take both sisters as wives."

Prairie Flower looked from Stands Tall to Cougar and back, and all three women let a smile show and they began to laugh together. Prairie Flower shook her head and said, "I wonder what Red Hawk will say to this?" and again the three women laughed together.

13 / DESECRATION

The slow rising sun painted the bellies of the low-lying grey clouds that shrouded the eastern mountains, laying a pink cast on the rolling foothills and valleys below. Gabe and Spotted Eagle rode side by side, the early light of morning at their backs, stretching the shadows of the ridden horses before them. They stayed about twenty yards from the shoreline, keeping a good pace as Wolf trotted some distance ahead. Gabe glanced at Spotted Eagle, "So, looks like Red Hawk is gonna be takin' a woman as his own soon."

Eagle shook his head, grunted, and said, "He sees himself as a great warrior and hunter. He thinks it will be easy to provide for a family, but he will soon find it is not all warm nights in the buffalo robe."

"The way things are, it won't be too long 'fore his little brother, White Feather, follows Red Hawk."

"It makes me feel old." Eagle looked at his friend,

"Yours are little now, but soon they too will be making their own lodge."

"Hey! Don't go rushin' things! My oldest, Bobcat, is barely walkin' and you've already got him takin' a woman and buildin' a lodge! I am not ready for that!" declared Gabe, chuckling with Eagle.

As the trail bent around the east end of the big bay that held the islands, the sun warmed their right shoulders, but as they followed the shoreline and turned east, they had to shade their eyes from the brilliance of the morning sun. But a little more than two miles and the trail bent to the north and Eagle pointed to the basin that sat back away from the shoreline, "We have camped here before," indicating the wide basin, "but the graze is better where we are and we will return here in a year or two." It was the way of the people to care for the land and to vary their camps so as not to overgraze or destroy the terrain with the impact of two or three hundred people and twice that many horses spending several months depleting the resources, firewood, graze for the animals and the plants used for food and medicines.

It was late morning when they rounded the point south of the site of the Kutenai encampment. The site was still a little more than a mile distant, but the desecration was evident even from a distance. Surprisingly, a small tendril of smoke rose from the midst of the black scars that marked where lodges had once stood. The men reined up, looked at the scene, then nudged their horses forward. As they neared, some of the many carrion eaters scattered. Turkey Buzzards flapped lazy wings to lift off, make a low circle and return to the grisly feast. Ravens argued with eagles, coyotes scampered among the dead snatching mouthfuls on the run, badgers hissed at bobcats, and two wolves tore at the carcass of a horse. The stench of death, burned flesh, and other refuse was overwhelming and Gabe lifted his neckerchief to cover his nose as Eagle tucked his face into his tunic.

They rode among the desolation, seeing mutilated bodies, stripped and scalped, lodges with tipi poles partially burned, hide covers burned, tule mat covers destroyed, and a veritable convention of carrion eaters. Gabe looked at Spotted Eagle, "Do we try to bury the bodies?"

"Where?" asked Eagle, waving his arm around to indicate the terrain. "We cannot dig a hole big enough, we cannot put them in the water . . ." he looked around, shaking his head, "Their spirits have crossed over, the animals are feasting, what more can we do?"

"What if we were to pile them together, put the tipi poles and brush atop, and burn them?"

Eagle frowned, looking around and considering what could be done, then pointed to a low spot that led between a high ridge and a low knob, "There."

They went to work, Gabe using a long hemp

rope they used to secure packs, Eagle with a braided rawhide rope. They dragged body after body, some partial bodies that had been ripped apart by carrion eaters, and anything that would easily burn, making a sizable pile. Lastly, they dragged the partially burned tipi poles and lay them across the pile and brush and started the fire. They stood back, watching the flames lick at the brush and debris, then turned to look at the other stacks they had made, assorted and partially burned hide covers, blankets, buffalo robes and anything else that might be salvageable.

They looked at one another and Gabe said, “I found some yucca root soap, so I’m gonna try to wash some o’ this stench off!” and started to the water’s edge, leading Ebony with Wolf following. He ground tied the big black, motioned to Wolf to lay down, then lay his hawk and pistol on the saddle seat and waded into the water. Eagle watched, and soon followed. They sudsed their buckskins thoroughly, Gabe his tunic and britches, Eagle his leggings and breechcloth, and washed their hair and bodies, rinsed, and started to the shore but were stopped by the figure of an old man, standing and staring at the two. His grey hair was matted with blood on the side of his head, dried blood showed at his hip and leg, he leaned on a long stick and frowned at the two men.

“You are not Blackfoot!” he signed, grunting with the effort.

Gabe and Eagle came from the water, Eagle signing to the old man, "No, I am Salish, he," pointing to Gabe with his chin, "is a friend. Your women and children are at our camp beyond the island."

The old man nodded, his expression changeless, and slowly lowered himself to the ground. Gabe spoke softly to Eagle, "His wounds need to be tended."

Eagle nodded, signed to the man, "May we look at your wounds? And you can tell us of the raid by the Blackfoot."

Within a short while, the men had washed, applied poultices and bandages, and sat beside the old man who said his name was Moccasin Track. "I was looking for camas root. My woman crossed over a long time past, I must find my own camas. When the Blackfoot attacked, they came from there," motioning to the trees that shadowed the west edge of the village, "and there," pointing to the ridge on the east edge. "I was there, across the water." He pointed at the narrow finger bay that pushed into the north shore and lay below the camp. "I could do nothing, but I tried to come back, and was beaten with a war club by one man. I crawled into the brush to die, but the Creator would not take me."

Gabe looked at Eagle, "How 'bout us gettin' away from the stink, maybe back yonder a ways, get us somethin' to eat and then decide what we'll do next."

Eagle nodded, and went to his horse, motioned for

the old man to come with him, swung aboard and helped Moccasin Track up to sit behind him. Gabe swung aboard Ebony and with Wolf in the lead, they moved away from the camp, around the point and went to a grassy flat with a smattering of fir and ponderosa for shade and stepped down. Gabe had some biscuits with strips of venison from last night's meal, handed one to each of the two, Moccasin Track and Eagle, and they sat down to look across the lake and enjoy the bit of food. Gabe was thinking how good a cup of coffee would taste when Eagle said, "The council said I was to report back about the village."

"Umhmm, and the old man here can't stay by himself, so, I was thinkin' maybe you could take him back with you and I'll follow the Blackfoot, see what they're up to."

Eagle frowned, "Why?"

Gabe snorted, laughed, "Dunno. Just seems like I oughta. Cougar did tell the women we'd try to get the horses back and I figger it might be a good idea to know where the Blackfoot are headed, how many there are, you know. What if they decided to come back and try to take our village again?"

"You are one man. There are at least two double hands of the Blackfoot."

"I ain't plannin' on takin' 'em on. Just scout 'em out. Shouldn't take more'n two, three days." He looked at Eagle, "But if you're worried about me, you could always bring Ezra and maybe a couple others and follow along after."

Eagle shook his head, looking down at the ground between his feet, then looked back at Gabe, "Black Buffalo said you always find trouble wherever you go."

Gabe grinned, "I know, he's like that. He worries about me like he was my mother or somethin'." Gabe finished his tasty tidbit and went to Ebony, tightened the girth, watched Eagle as he mounted and helped Moccasin Track aboard, then mounted the big stallion and grinned at Eagle, "I'll be back soon," He reined Ebony around to return to the wide trail left by the Blackfoot and the herd of stolen horses. Wolf trotted beside Ebony as they rounded the point and Gabe waved over his shoulder to Eagle and Moccasin Track.

He had been riding the high side of the wide trail when he spotted the tracks of a lone rider that came from the edge of the trees to join the tracks of the herd. Gabe paused, leaned down to look at the tracks, saw a nick in the left front hoof and remembered the sign left at the scene of the attack on the Salish village where he and Red Hawk confronted the Blackfoot. One rider who was wounded and lay on the neck of his horse as he retreated, had left the trail. Gabe remembered seeing this same track and knew this was the wounded warrior from the point. He lifted his eyes along the wide trail, reckoning the band was traveling north, away from the lake but parallel to the west bank.

He stood in his stirrups, looking all around, thinking, *Now, Cougar said the land of the Blackfoot was to the east, so if they're headin' home, they would need to turn east after they reach the north shore of the lake. Reckon I'll just follow 'em far 'nuff to see if they're goin' back to their country, or up to more mischief.*

14 / FOLLOW

The two scouts, Kicking Horse and Stands Alone, rode from the trees to join the band driving the herd. White Eagle and Elk Child rode together with Red Crow near and all three stopped to await the two scouts. Eagle motioned to the rest of the warriors to stop the herd and to let them graze in the flat below the ridge. "The village is as you said," began Kicking Horse. "There are two double hands of lodges, the horse herd is less, but graze away from the village." Eagle nodded, "Warriors?"

"We saw several, but none that showed they were readying for a hunt or raid," stated Stands Alone.

"You know that how?" asked Elk Child.

"None were working on weapons; we saw no weapons. Some worked on nets, but not weapons."

When White Eagle led his raiding party from their village, they had purposely swung wide to go around this village without being detected. His plan was to take this smaller village on their way back from their first choice. If they were successful, which they were, with the first attack, this would be an easy fight and would add to their bounty. The men's spirits would be high and they would be anxious for more. Both villages were Kutenai and the Blackfoot saw them as an easy target.

Red Crow had come close to hear the report of the scouts and watched and listened as White Eagle spoke with his closest warrior and favored leader, Elk Child. The two men looked at one another grinning and Elk Child said, "It will be an easy victory, as you planned."

Crow moved closer, "This is the village you said you would take?"

Eagle scowled at his rival, nodded curtly, and turned back to the scouts. "Return to the ridge, one of you go over and watch from the far side, the other from this side. We will take the herd to the head of the valley beyond the first ridge with the tall hill. We will camp there and you can return after dark."

The scouts reined their mounts around and started to the trees as Red Crow turned to White Eagle and asked, "Will you make plans when we camp?"

"The plan is already made. We will attack at first light like we did with the last fight. We had a victory, you were defeated. If you stay, you will do as we say," declared White Eagle, then gigged his horse away, allowing no argument from Red Crow.

***

Gabe leaned low to examine the tracks of the Blackfoot. They were moving at a good pace, but not hurried. That told they had no concern about being followed. He sat up, stood in his stirrups to look down the trail, obvious in the late afternoon light, and noticed they appeared to be moving further away from the shore of the lake, bearing to the northwest and into the low hills. He frowned as he considered their direction, puzzled at the change. He nudged Ebony on, staying on the uphill side of the trail, nearer the thicker trees and often had to wend his way through the thicker timber.

When he came to a wide blowdown with the terrain littered with weathered dead trees and standing snags all tangled with the standing and new growth pine, he moved out of the trees and nearer the trail. He could tell by the sign he was gaining on the band and kept a sharp lookout on the trail ahead, being careful not to come upon them unexpectedly. It would be common practice for a war party to have one of their number hang back to watch their back trail for any sign of pursuit or giveaway, but Gabe had been watchful and saw no sign of any warriors moving apart from the others, but he remained vigilant.

A quick glance to the lowering sun prompted him to lift a hand to measure the remaining daylight, quickly calculating by the number of fingers above the horizon, there was less than a half hour before the sun dropped below the western mountains. Another hour and a half or so of dusk and twilight, then darkness. But he knew the moon had been waxing to full and believed there would be ample light to continue his tracking, if he felt it necessary. But first, he would give Ebony a breather, himself something to eat and all of them a rest.

The trail took a sudden turn and ducked into a cut between a low timber covered knob and a high ridge marked by a tall sparsely timbered round top. The sign showed the horse herd was strung out and went over a low saddle crossing that crested the ridge with the round top. Gabe glanced at the sun, then the crest and slowed. His hackles were up at the back of his neck and he moved Ebony into a thick cluster of tall fir and stepped down. He loosely tethered the big stallion, motioned Wolf to stay with Ebony, then with his scope in hand, he started to the crest of the ridge, paused, and returned to put his belt pistol, the over/under double barreled Bailes, in his saddle bags. He frowned at his own actions but had followed his inclinations and started back to the crest.

He moved on the low side of the ridge, staying in the trees and leaving no sign among the long pine needles of the ponderosa or the matted leaves of the quakies. Once near the east edge of the tall round top, he worked his way to the crest, careful to stay in heavy cover. As he neared the crest, he went to a crouch beside some oak brush, then bellied down and moved cautiously to the edge. Even without the scope, he could see the big herd milling in the clearing of the low basin between the ridges. He watched, first searching the nearby trees and rocks for any sign of a lookout and satisfied he was alone, he stretched out the brass scope, shielding the end with his hand to prevent the lowering sun from reflecting off the lens.

The Blackfoot were making camp, rolling out their bedrolls, watching over the horses, but Gabe also noticed they made no moves to have a fire. Gabe frowned, *If they don't have any fires, they must be plannin' somethin' soon, must be somethin' near,* he thought. He watched the war party a little longer, saw no movement to send scouts or to post lookouts. He frowned, then crabbed back from the crest, changing his position to look around by the waning light. The sun was painting the western sky with bold colors that fringed the heavy clouds and sent lances across the sky.

Gabe sat below the crest and moved the scope along the far ridge, following the slope to the water's edge where the ridge dropped abruptly to a low cut, leaving a cluster of small humps that pushed into the water. But it was the far side of those humps that caught Gabe's attention, the ends of tipi poles stood above the irregular terrain and gave away the presence of a village. Gabe scanned the area, guessing the village to number about twenty lodges, not a big village, but enough to have a good number of warriors, as many as sixty to seventy or so, but not as big as the other village of the Kutenai already destroyed by this same band of Blackfoot. He could tell it was probably another village of Kutenai by the tule mat covered tipis that stood among the hide tipis. This was a people that lived among the wetlands and were at home along the rivers.

Gabe turned to look back at the Blackfoot camp, saw no change, then with another glance at the village, he shook his head at what he knew he had to do, somehow he had to warn the village of the probable Blackfoot attack. He slid down from the edge, came to his feet, and went to the trees where Ebony and Wolf waited. It would be after dark when he rode into the camp, and he was a complete stranger, didn't speak their language and knew his only way would be with sign, and he would also have to tell them about the other village raided by the Blackfoot.

He stepped aboard, stuck the pistol in his belt and started through the trees, remembering the trail he saw from up top and pushed Ebony toward that trail. As he dropped from the thick timber, he crossed the trail of two horses and paused. He considered and guessed these were scouts sent ahead to watch the village. He stayed behind cover, shielding himself from any scout that might be on high ground. As he neared the encampment, dusk still offered enough light for him to be seen well before he was too close. He rode with one hand high, his weapons holstered, and speaking softly in the Salish tongue, hoping someone would understand. Several warriors appeared on either side, lances and bows threatening, but he kept moving, repeating, "I am a friend."

As he entered the village, three men stood before him, the warriors staying beside him, but shying away from Wolf who stayed close to Ebony. Gabe reined up and spoke, "I am a friend. I am called Spirit Bear and I come with a warning for you."

The men before him looked askance, obviously not understanding, and Gabe slowly lowered his hand and began signing. "I am a friend. I am with the Salish, camped below the lake. I come to tell you of the Blackfoot."

The expression 'Blackfoot' got their attention, causing them to look from one to another and back to Gabe. He continued, "There is a war party of Blackfoot camped at the head of that valley," he motioned behind him between the two ridges, "That party attacked and destroyed another village of the Kutenai. The warriors of the Kutenai were all killed, the women and children escaped and are now with the Salish. I believe the Blackfoot are going to attack your village at first light." His warning startled the warriors and the three who stood before him that were obviously the leaders of the village.

"Why do you tell us this?" asked the older of the three leaders.

"An old man, Moccasin Track, still lives and is with the Salish. The Salish are my friends, and the Kutenai are friends with the Salish."

"Will you stay and fight with us?" asked another of the leaders.

Gabe shook his head, "I will go back to see if I can do something to stop the attack."

"What can one man do?"

"I do not know, but I must try," answered Gabe. He looked at the leaders and at the warriors, then added, "These are fierce fighters. With their number, maybe two double hands of warriors, they destroyed the village below and that village was much larger than yours. You must be ready and fight well."

The men looked at one another and the leader looked at Gabe, "We are grateful to Spirit Bear. May the Spirit of the Creator ride with you."

"And with you," answered Gabe as he reined around, resigned to his task, whatever it might be, but he knew he had to do what he could, for he could not allow another village to be desecrated by the fearsome Blackfoot. He thought, *It seems like everywhere we go, we run into some Blackfoot that are bent on destroying everything and everyone they find.*

15 / DISCOVERED

Gabe swung wide of the valley where the Blackfoot were camped with their herd of stolen horses, taking the south side of the broad ridge with the big round top knoll. He looked to the night sky, the almost full moon giving ample light for the trail, but he noted the scattered cloud cover and knew he would appreciate the clouds masking the brightness of the moon when he made his move. He stayed near the edge of the trees, using the thick woods to mask any sound of his movement, and pushed Ebony to the base of the round top, where a broad swath of black timber would be suitable to leave his horse. At the lower edge of the timber, mostly tall skinny fir and towering ponderosa, a basin of tall grass offered ample graze for a tired Ebony. He found a spot with tall green grass and the shelter of a big ponderosa and stepped down.

He loosely tethered Ebony to a fir sapling, confident in his ability to pull free if threatened and stood beside the big black, resting his forearms on the seat of the saddle, thinking. He knew he was about a mile, as the crow flies, from the Blackfoot camp. He chuckled as he thought of that phrase, remembering reading it in some review of English Literature when he attended the college at Philadelphia. He shook his head and brought his thoughts back to the present, glanced down at Wolf and absentmindedly stroked the neck of Ebony. As he considered, he thought *Maybe if I do something with the horse herd, stampede 'em, maybe. But there will be lookouts . . .* He considered the layout of the camp, where the herd was kept, and what he might do to use the herd to his advantage. He glanced at Wolf again, he had bellied down beside the big black and looked up at Gabe, waiting for him to move or something, and Gabe looked at Ebony. *If I take Ebony, the horses might smell him coming, whinny and give us away, and if I take Wolf, they will smell wolf and be spooked, thinking a pack might attack.* He shook his head, knowing what he must do and not liking his options.

He bent down and stroked Wolf's scruff, spoke softly to him, "You stay. You stay with Ebony. I'll be back. Alright boy?" He rubbed behind the big wolf's ears, stood, and stroked Ebony's face, "I'll be back soon." He slipped the belt pistol free, stuffed it, his powder horn and possibles bag, in the saddle bags and checked his knives that hung at his back between his shoulder blades, slipped them back in the sheaths, felt his tomahawk at his belt, and started to the trees.

He moved silently through the trees, shafts of moonlight piercing the canopy of pines and lighting his way. He stayed in the trees but moved on the shoulder that fell from the crest of the ridge, following a dry wash that, if it were earlier in the season, would probably be carrying spring runoff, but now held only deep shadows. As he neared the crest of the ridge, he slowed, went to a crouch and eased his way to the top. Keeping a scraggly fir between him and the basin that held the horse herd, he searched the shadows for the lookouts that would be watching the herd. He breathed easy, unmoving, scanning the grassy basin and the trees on the downhill side.

He slowly lowered himself to his haunches, a move that would usually be done in an instant and with one fluid move, but he knew any movement, even in the dim moonlight, would catch the eye of anyone watching. He seated himself beside the tree trunk, leaned back against it and watched. As he waited, a dark cloud moved across the face of the moon, bringing a span of deep darkness across the valley bottom. Gabe glanced at the sky, watched the cloud for a moment, then looked at the basin and the horse herd, knowing the cloud would soon unmask the moon and he could catch movement and the lookouts would feel relief at the lifting of the darkness and move. He waited.

As he sat in the shadow of the rough barked fir, he lifted his eyes to peer through the thin limbs and saw the cloud moving slowly across the face of the moon, then looked at the basin. He watched the edge of the cloud's shadow give way and move through the treetops, reminding him of the rising of the curtain on a stage, but the drama on this stage would be one of life and death. As the shadow touched the tree line, Gabe saw movement, just a slight step, of a lookout that stood, wrapped in a blanket at the edge of the grassy meadow. Gabe marked the place by the trees, then scanned across the edge, there! The second watcher was sitting horseback, hunkered down also with a blanket, probably snoozing as he sat aboard his mount. The horse stood three legged and head down, unmoving. As the shadow moved across the basin, he saw two more guards on the lower end, near the trees, also mounted, but unmoving.

Gabe felt the chill of the night air, shivered from his inaction, and moved back into the trees before standing. He judged it to be just before midnight, and with a quick glance to the heavens, saw the cloud cover growing heavier, but the big moon shone through some, sent lances of light through others, just enough to give light to move, but darkness for cover. He would have good cover down the face of the ridge, but it grew sparse at the base and offered nothing but buck brush and berry bushes.

As the trees allowed, he flitted from shadow to shadow, never exposing himself to any light, and made his way to the bottom of the ridge at the upper end of the meadow. Now he would have to go to his belly and his movement would have to mimic that of a slug, a slow one at that and he could leave no trail that might be discovered by a scout that could be moving about.

The tall grass was damp with the night dew and Gabe's buckskins were soon heavy with the moisture, but the wetness darkened his buckskins and muffled his movements. When a dry covering would cause a slight whisper, the dampness was silent. He crawled slowly nearer the first watchman. A distance that could be covered in seconds with the long strides of the man, now stretched before him, as he pushed through the grass covering only inches with each move. He guarded his breathing, for in the night, every sound is amplified and with little or no night sounds to cover it, he cautiously inhaled and exhaled through his nose. His eyes began to burn with the strain, but he saw the blanket wrapped shadow before him and he moved to his left to put the tree between them. As he came closer to the trees, the grass gave way to deep long ponderosa needles and Gabe knew if they were damp, he could move silently, but if he stepped on a dry cone or a thick pile of dry needles, it would be a giveaway.

As he brought up one knee, he reached to his back to slip the larger Flemish knife from its sheath, and with one hand on the pine needles, he brought up his second knee and slowly rose to a crouch. He watched the blanket shrouded man leaning back against the tree and noted his even breathing which told Gabe the man was asleep. Gabe lifted one foot, stretched it forward, shifted his weight, and then the other. He was within reach of the man and gave a quick glance in the direction of the second guard, saw nothing and brought his gaze back before him. He purposely did not look directly at the man, knowing the tendency of the mind to tell one when someone is staring at them. Another step and he reached out with his left hand, instantly covering the man's mouth, and jerking his head against the rough bark of the tree trunk, and with the knife in his right hand, slit the man's throat side to side. Blood spurted out on the blade and hand of Gabe, but he held tight as the man squirmed, grabbing at the hand that held him, until he kicked and went slack and still. Gabe lowered the man to the side, pulled the blanket free and lay it aside, then moved the man back to a sitting position against the tree. He picked up the blanket, folding it over one arm as he looked to the horses. He saw a couple with heads lifted and looking his direction, but they soon dropped their noses to the grass and took a few steps nearer the other horses and grew still. Gabe moved quietly away from the body and went deeper into the trees.

He paused a moment, leaned against a tall ponderosa, and caught his breath, stilled his nerves, and started in the direction of the second guard. As he neared the mounted guard, he stayed in the deep shadows, watching until he was satisfied the guard was still snoozing, trusting his mount to give any needed warning. Gabe moved until he was in line behind the guard and slowly started his stalk, uncertain of how he could take this one without causing an alarm. The pine needles quieted his movements, but the distance of twenty yards still took him a quarter hour to cover. As he neared, the horse shifted his weight, rocking the lookout, but not waking him. Gabe stood still and silent, waiting for the even breathing that would tell of sleep. The man sat, head hanging, blanket over his head, and unmoving.

Gabe moved closer, went to the left side, keeping the horse and rider between him and the herd and the guards on the lower end of the meadow. When he was near, he lunged forward, jumping up with the tomahawk held high and as he brought the hawk down at the neck of the man, he grabbed the rein with his left hand. As the hawk plunged into the man's neck, it severed the spinal cord, killing him instantly and as Gabe had the rein, the horse spooked, but was quickly pulled around as Gabe pulled the rider to the ground. The horse was skittish with the smell of blood and the strange smell of the white man, but Gabe spoke softly and stroked the animal's neck, calming him.

He looked to the lower end of the meadow, saw one of the mounted guards moving as if he was coming to check on this man, and Gabe snatched the blanket from the rider and swung back aboard the horse, wrapping the blanket around his shoulders, and calming the animal as he backed him into the shadows. Gabe looked at the other guards, one unmoving the other turning his mount back to the point where he had been, apparently satisfied with Gabe appearing as the guard of the upper end of the meadow. Gabe breathed easy, relaxing for a few moments, considering his next move.

He watched the clouds covering the big moon, then break apart and let a glimmer of light through, until the next cloud dropped its covering over the night lantern. The moon was high in the sky, showing it to be just past midnight, and the stars were dancing high above the scattered cover. There was no breeze, but the air was cool, and Gabe took a moment to warm himself in the stolen blanket, knowing that this blanket probably came from the lodge of the Kutenai and he shook his head at the remembrance. He ground his teeth as he clenched and unclenched his jaw, the muscles in his shoulders, neck, and jaw tight with anticipation. He muttered a simple prayer for God's hand to be upon him and let the blanket slide from his shoulders as he readied himself.

16 / STAMPEDE

Gabe quickly scanned the horse herd, pulled the blanket from behind him and started to the right, choosing to start the herd moving slowly. He pushed his mount to the edge, turning the horses away from him, then moved further to his right to start the others in the same direction. As the herd began to bunch up at the back, he saw the two guards at the lower end start to move. Gabe grabbed the blanket, shook it out at his side, then lifted and snapped it up and popped it, shouting and screaming at the same time, "EEEEeeeyaaaahhhh! Hiiiyaeeee!!" as loud as he could. He grasped his mount tight with his legs, digging his heels into the ribs, and used both hands to wave and pop the blanket. He grabbed a handful of mane and screamed again, "Eeeyaaahhh! Whoooeeeee Horse!" His own mount lunged forward again, tried to hunch his back to buck, but Gabe pulled on the reins, jerking his head up and drove the horse at the back of the herd.

The animals lunged together as if joined as one, some reared up, tossing their heads, and pawing at the clouds. Several whickered and whinnied, screaming their surprise as the herd leapt into a driving stampede. Dirt clods flew, horses shouldered into each other, some kicking back at those behind, pandemonium ensued as the herd of over a hundred horses drove for the break in the trees. Gabe saw the two guard's horses stumble as they sought to turn with the herd, then he lost sight. He was screaming, shouting, and waving the blanket, driving the horses before him. The leaders of the herd drove through the trees, stampeding into the camp of the Blackfoot raiders, scattering them like so many prairie dogs scrambling to their holes as a pack of hungry wolves chased after. Some dove behind trees, others shook blankets at the horses, trying to turn the herd aside. Within moments, Gabe, still screaming and waving the blanket, charged through the first warriors, hearing them shouting and seeing them dive for cover. He tossed the blanket aside, lay low on the horse's neck and reined him to the middle of the camp and into the herd itself, trying to obscure himself from the Blackfoot.

Gabe slapped his legs to his mount, leaning far forward, a handful of mane his anchor. He squinted through the flying mane that slapped at his face, trying to see in the dim light of the shadowed moon, following hard after the scattered herd. He saw a downed horse, flailing on its back, hooves pawing the air, one broken leg flopping. He jerked on the reins to pull his mount to the side and miss the injured animal, but his horse stumbled, caught its balance, and tossed his head, screamed, and fell on its neck and chest, catapulting Gabe over his head.

With a handful of ripped out mane in one hand, the end of the rein in the other, Gabe found himself flying end over end through the darkness. He stretched out his foot to find the ground, but he tumbled over, caught a glimpse of the edge of the moon that appeared to wink at him, then the empty blackness of the ground rushed up to meet him as he landed face first, knocking the wind out of him and rendering him unconscious. As the black curtain lowered over his eyes, he gasped for air, but none was coming. He saw black, red, and nothing.

Gabe felt air filling his lungs and he tried to breathe deeper, but pain stabbed at his side. He winced at the hurt as another pounded at his head and a searing jabbed at his hip, but he had yet to open his eyes. He tried to move his arms, realized they were outstretched, felt pain in his shoulders, and tried to lift his knees, but was stopped by the bindings at his ankles. He breathed deep, pulled lightly at his wrists, and felt the rawhide dig into his flesh. Whenever he was awakened, he would never move anything but his eyes, searching his surroundings first and needing to know what was about. The habit stayed with him as he opened his eyes just a slit, and the brightness of daylight stabbed into his eyes, making him close them tighter still.

He did his best to check his ability to move, his fingers worked, nothing felt broken other than maybe some ribs, the dull thudding in his head lessened and he carefully measured his breath and tried again to open his eyes a slit. The sun was well up, so he must have been unconscious for several hours and he was bound, spread eagled and on the ground. As he moved slightly, he was surprised to feel his knives were still in the sheath at his back, undiscovered by the Blackfoot. But they had no reason to think anyone would carry a weapon in such a place, for warriors always had their weapons ready at hand at their waist. He squinted again and saw a group of warriors seated near the trees and another man staked out on the ground nearby. One of the warriors stared at him, scowling, then shouted to someone across the camp.

The group of warriors stood and started toward Gabe, so he slowly opened his eyes and moved his head slightly to look around. He saw three other warriors striding toward him, scowling at him as they neared. The leader of the second group wore a tall porcupine roach with feathers at the back and every move was accented by the shaking of the roach. He came close, leaned over to look at Gabe, his eyes flaring, and his lip snarling and he growled. He stood up, looking at the others and shouted, "This one lives! We will see if he can die like a man or if he whines like a dog or squirms like a snake! Aiiieeee!" White Eagle lifted his lance to the sky, dropped his head and moved as if he was dancing.

Another man leaned over to look at Gabe as he lay stretched out and bound. He turned and shouted to the first man, "This man killed our warriors when we attacked the Salish! I demand my right to kill him!"

Gabe understood the tongue of the Blackfoot and knew their intent. The second man with his buffalo scalp horned headdress looked familiar and when he told the others of the Salish attack, Gabe knew this was the one that fled when the others were killed.

White Eagle glared at Red Crow, "You saw this man at the Salish camp?"

"When we attacked, he was among the many that ambushed my band and killed the others. After I killed three, perhaps more, was when my horse spooked and ran! I saw this man with the Salish and saw him kill our warriors! I demand the right to fight him to the death!"

Another warrior, Kicking Horse, stepped forward, "It is the way of our people! When one who has been wounded demands the right, it must be given him. But this man killed my brother, Big Horn, who watched over the horses. If Red Crow does not kill him, I claim that right!"

The other warriors shouted and screamed their war cries, wanting to see their warriors kill this man who almost stopped their raid on the Kutenai village. As Gabe looked around, he saw two women, bound and tied to a tree, and with another glance at the other man that was spread-eagled and bound nearby, he knew they were Kutenai, which meant the village had been raided and probably destroyed and these taken captive.

White Eagle glared at Red Crow, glanced at Kicking Horse, and looked at Gabe. He walked toward the white man, snarled at he looked at him, mumbled, "It is our way that this man shall die." He motioned to two of the warriors to cut his bonds and they cautiously came near, cut the bindings at his feet and each man put a knee on an arm, then cut the rawhides at his wrists. When they stepped back, knives held out before them, Gabe slowly sat up, rubbing his wrists and then his ankles. He looked at White Eagle, then spoke in the tongue of the Blackfoot, "Am I to fight that coward?" nodding toward Red Crow.

Eagle frowned and stepped back as Red Crow lunged forward, "I will kill you!" but Eagle stopped him. White Eagle looked at Gabe, "You know our tongue and you call him a coward. Why?"

"I heard him say a big band of Salish ambushed him and his men, and he killed three Salish before his horse ran away." Gabe chuckled, shaking his head, "He came with this many," he held out six fingers, "and he was hiding behind the leaders. There were two of us, one young Salish warrior in the brush, and I stood in the middle of the trail and warned them they would die if they came, and they did!" He glared at Red Crow, "This man did not kill any, but the arrow from the young warrior cut his shoulder and he screamed and fled like a woman!"

"Aiiieeee!" screamed Red Crow, lunging toward Gabe, his knife held blade up in his outstretched hand. Two others stepped before him, stopping him as White Eagle again held up his hand, looked at Gabe and then to Red Crow. He grinned at his arch rival, shook his head, and said, "This man killed five of our warriors and you ran away! It is only right that you must fight him now." He motioned to the other warriors to move Red Crow back and turned to face Gabe, "What are you called?"

"I am Spirit Bear!" declared Gabe.

"Spirit Bear," repeated White Eagle, nodding and grinning. "It is the way of our people that if a warrior believes he has been wronged, he can demand the right to fight that one. Red Crow has demanded that right."

Gabe nodded, "I also heard that one," pointing with his chin to Kicking Horse, "say he wanted to fight too. So, when I kill Red Crow, do I fight him."

White Eagle grinned, "We will decide that after this is settled," nodding toward the waiting Red Crow.

Gabe saw Crow with a hatchet in one hand, a knife in the other as he went to a crouch, glaring and snarling at the white man. Gabe looked at Eagle, "He has a tomahawk and a knife . . ."

"You fight with what you have!" declared White Eagle, grinning.

Gabe lifted his eyebrows, looked at Red Crow and asked, "You sure you want to do this?" holding his open hands to the side, grinning.

Crow glared, screamed his war cry, and charged.

Gabe had a quick thought, *"Oh what I'd do for my pistols right about now!"*

17 / BOUT

As Red Crow charged, he held his knife, blade up, in his right hand and the tomahawk in his left. As he neared Gabe he raised the hawk, but Gabe saw the move that was meant to gut him, the knife held low, so he feinted to his right, stepped quickly to the left and spun sideways, sucking in his stomach as the blade slipped past, narrowly missing his buckskin tunic. Gabe moved quickly, hooking his foot in front of Red Crow's, bending to the left away from him and driving his elbow down into the back of Crow, tripping him as he fell forward and driving him face down into the ground. Gabe stepped lithely back, dropped into a crouch to wait for Crow to rise.

Crow quickly rolled to his side and came to his feet, slapping the dirt from his face with his forearm, and spinning around, looking for Gabe. Gabe grinned, said, "Over here, Crow!" and gave him the come-on sign with both open hands extended from his sides. The Blackfoot warrior snarled, warily moving side to side, watching Gabe, expecting the white man to lunge at him, but Gabe just waited, shifting his weight from one foot to the other, keeping his eyes on Crow's. Red Crow flinched as a bit of dirt fell from his buffalo scalp headdress, and he snatched at it and tossed it aside.

Crow moved in a crouch, side stepping, trying to make Gabe move in a circle, but Gabe never lifted his feet as he shifted side to side, watching. Crow feinted with the knife, followed it quickly with a wide swing from the tomahawk and Gabe leaned back away from the swing. But as it passed his chest, Gabe dropped his right hand on the wrist of Crow, slapped up with his left hand and clasped the wrist/forearm of Red Crow in both hands putting his thumbs on the back of his hand and lifted it high with the palm facing Red Crow, who looked up at the tomahawk still in his hand, when Gabe suddenly brought the wrist of Crow down, still clasping it tightly, and as it came even with the man's waist, the snap of the bone could be heard by everyone nearby.

Red Crow screamed with the pain of his arm breaking and Gabe released the arm, stepped back as Crow dropped the tomahawk from his useless hand, put the knife's blade between his teeth as he grabbed at his broken wrist with his free hand. He glared at Gabe, eyes wide and snarled as he growled through clenched teeth. Gabe stepped back, shrugged, and dropped into his crouch, waiting for the man to make a move.

Anger drove Red Crow and he grabbed the knife from his teeth, stuffed his left hand in his belt at his stomach, and with his knife held blade up, he scowled at Gabe and feinted again and again with the knife, but Gabe watched the man's eyes, knowing they would giveaway his moves. The man shifted side to side, glowering at his opponent, his upper lip twitching as his nostrils flared and his eyes squinted. He lunged forward, arm outstretched, and Gabe dropped to the ground, making Crow think he stumbled and fell, but as the man rushed at him, Gabe swept his feet from under him with a swing of his leg, dropping Crow flat on his back, knocking the wind from him. As he gasped for air, he rolled to the side, wincing as he nudged his broken arm, and slowly came to his feet.

Crow moved slower, more cautiously, watching Gabe's every move, realizing he was in the fight of his life. He rocked side to side, shuffling his feet, feinted to his right, making Gabe step slightly to his left and Crow brought the knife in a sweeping arc at Gabe's midriff. Gabe sucked in his gut, hands high, as he tried to step back and felt the cut of the blade as it sliced through his buckskin tunic and drew blood. Gabe stepped back as Crow caught his balance and started another lunge, but Gabe brought a wide hammer blow with both hands clasped together, and smashed Red Crows nose, splattering blood across his face and neck, blinding him for a moment. Gabe pressed his advantage and grabbed the wrist of the knife holding hand, pulled Crow forward, pivoted, and did a rolling hip block and threw the man over his shoulder to land flat of his back. Gabe lunged forward, snatched the knife from his fingers, and held it to Red Crow's throat.

Gabe looked to White Eagle and the other warriors, all of whom stood silent and staring, then back to White Eagle, who snarled and turned away. Gabe asked the warriors, "Should he die?"

All of them turned their back and Gabe looked at Red Crow, "This is for the Kutenai and the Salish people!" and pressed the knife to his throat, ready to slit it, until Red Crow pleaded, "No, I would live!"

Gabe was surprised. He had never heard a warrior beg for his life, but he chose to spare the man. He lessened the pressure, then stood, casting the knife to the side. He watched as a humbled Red Crow struggled to stand, wincing at the pain of his broken arm, then turned his back to Crow to face White Eagle. He nodded toward Kicking Horse, "Is he next?"

Kicking Horse stepped forward, a slight hesitation in his movement as he looked to White Eagle and said, "It is my right!"

White Eagle looked from Kicking Horse to Gabe,

then suddenly snatched his tomahawk from his belt and brought it up and back and threw it toward Gabe, but Gabe stepped to the side and the hawk flew by, and with a thunk that sounded like a horse kicking down a fence post, its head was buried in the skull of Red Crow, dropping him to his back as he dropped his knife. He had started a lunge behind Gabe, seeking to drive the knife in the white man's back, when the hawk of White Eagle stopped him. Gabe glanced back at the man, then turned to look at White Eagle, nodded and shook his head slightly. "You just can't trust some people."

Eagle stood somber faced, glaring at the white man and said, "It is the way of my people." He looked from Gabe to Kicking Horse and said, "We will do the run. Choose two warriors to join you." He looked at Gabe and said, "You will run, Kicking Horse and two others will come after you. You will have the length of a bow shot before one man follows. The same with each one. There will be three. They will try to kill you, but if you kill them, you are free and will no longer be sought."

"Sounds fair," answered Gabe, then noticed a slight grin start at the corner of White Eagle's mouth. "But there's something else?"

"Yes. You will be without clothes or weapons."

Gabe's eyes flared in surprise, "Naked?"

"Or you could fight them here, all three. But, if you kill one or all, there are these that could claim the same right to fight to the death."

Gabe looked from White Eagle to the others and knew there would be no end to it, they would come against him one or more after another until he was so worn out he could not defend himself. The run would be his best chance, even if he were naked. He shook his head at the thought, looked at White Eagle and asked, "When?"

"Now," declared the war leader of the Blackfoot, grinning at the white man. He added, "You are a good warrior, it is sad that you will die today."

Gabe grinned as he shucked off his britches, "I ain't dead yet."

When he slipped the tunic over his head, White Eagle frowned at the lanyard around Gabe's shoulders that held the sheath with the Flemish knives at his back. Gabe slipped it off and handed it to the man, "I'll be comin' back for those," he stated as he watched White Eagle slip the larger of the knives from the sheath. He turned it over in his hands, admiring the craftsmanship and felt the blade, pleased with the sharp edge. He looked at Gabe, "If you come back, I will give these to you," smiling as he slipped the scabbard behind his belt.

Gabe stood before them, totally naked, appreciating the warmth of the mid-day sun, and watched as White Eagle motioned for one of the warriors to shoot an arrow down valley in the direction of the lake. Gabe watched the arrow arc high, wishing he had his Mongol bow that could send the arrow over four hundred yards instead of the less than one hundred this arrow flew. When it fell from its arc and stuck in the ground, White Eagle nodded to Gabe and motioned him to run.

Without another thought, Gabe stretched out his long legs and started across the wide clearing, knowing the arrow didn't even make it to the tree line just under a hundred yards distant, but he had already calculated what he would do, knowing it would not be what was expected. His long stride and practice pace enabled him to cover the short distance quickly, but he did not slow and kept going in a straight line, remembering the many times he and Ezra ran bare footed through the woods pretending they were the Iriquois Indians of the time. That thought kept his mind off his feet as he plodded through the grass, but he knew once he made the tree line, it would not be as easy.

Within a few strides, he ducked behind a cluster of scraggly fir, and started to the high timber covered knob that stood tall on the south ridge. He had to make it up and over that ridge, then down to the ravine beyond to the little basin where Ebony and Wolf waited. But he also knew the first warrior was Kicking Horse and he was driven by vengeance, determined to shed blood for blood, and Kicking Horse was well armed.

Gabe started up through the thick timber, wending his way among the blow downs and the undergrowth, struggling to make his way higher. He came to a downed tree that lay across his way, and started to climb over but slipped just as an arrow whispered past and stuck in the trunk of the grey log. Gabe dropped to his belly, scrambling under the tree and into the thicker timber. He stopped behind a tall ponderosa, catching his breath, and listening. The crashing of the running Kicking Horse was unmistakable, and Gabe knew he was still on his trail and coming fast. Gabe dropped to the ground, staying low and facing downhill, searched for the Blackfoot.

Kicking Horse made no effort at stealth, knowing the white man knew he was coming, and he was unarmed so he had no fear of being seen. He charged on, breathing heavy, as he fought his way through the broken branches and downed timber. Gabe crabbed to the side, quickly searched for a sizable limb, caught sight of one and stretched out to grab it. Another arrow whispered past, but it struck well away from where he crouched, and Gabe knew Kicking Horse was shooting at sounds.

Gabe took a deep breath, worked his way to another big ponderosa and came to his feet. He waited, listening, and heard the slow steps of the big man, crunching the twigs and pine needles, yet moving as quietly as possible. Gabe held his breath, and as he heard another step, he started his swing and stepped from behind the tree, striking the Blackfoot on the side of his head, knocking him to the ground. Gabe stepped over him, club lifted, and saw the side of the man's head split open, blood coming from his ears and the split skin. Gabe knew if he wasn't dead, he soon would be and without waiting, he began to strip the man of his leggings, breechcloth, and moccasins. He quickly donned his new attire, grabbed up Kicking Horse's bow, quiver, knife and tomahawk and started back through the trees, knowing the second warrior had gained ground on him when he stopped to strip his first kill.

18 / RUN

Every step was harder, his breath came in gasps as he trudged up the steep hillside. The timber was dense, and he had to move at an angle across the face of the round top mountain, fighting his way through the close growing aspen and windfall from the pines. It was impossible to move silently, every step a giveaway of his presence, his raspy breathing tearing at his throat. Gabe stumbled against a tall ponderosa, grabbed at the low branch to keep from falling, his trembling legs giving out, dropping him to his knees. He looked at his backtrail, caught a brief glimpse of the nearest Blackfoot and forced himself behind the tree. He pulled himself up, nocked an arrow and leaned against the gnarly bark of the ponderosa and waited.

Gabe sucked air, his lungs raw and the pain from the broken ribs felt like a knife driving into his lower chest. He measured his breathing, needful of all the oxygen he could get, the thin mountain air starving him. He dug deep for more resolve and strength, peered around the tree, showing only the side of his face, saw the warrior stumbling up the timbered slope and lifted the bow to take aim. He waited for the man to step into the opening between the aspen and the pines, then let the arrow fly.

Gabe was used to his Mongol bow with its draw weight close to a hundred pounds, and the speed of the arrow much greater, but the stolen bow from the downed Blackfoot warrior was a typical bow of the plains tribes and had a draw weight of less than half the Mongol. Accordingly, Gabe's aim was off and the arrow narrowly missed his pursuer and fluttered behind him, but it prompted the man to drop to the ground to take cover behind some undergrowth. Gabe nocked another arrow and waited, knowing the impatience of the warrior would drive the man to make a move, and he did. Gabe's arrow flew true, taking the man in the upper thigh and dropping him to the ground.

Gabe instantly turned and leaned into the steep hill, digging his toes deep and driving himself upwards. Often using his hand and fingers to stay upright as he pumped his legs against the almost vertical climb, he often grabbed at tufts of grass and rocks for added leverage. One step, push, lift, another step, push, pull, drive, another step, breathe, push, and looking up, he saw the daylight of the crest. Just a little ways further. He grabbed at the scraggly branch of a mountain mahogany; a quick glance of the stubby tree showed the seeds that prompted the natives to call it the 'Fuzzy Tail'.

Gabe made a quick survey of his surroundings, looking for a place of cover to wait for the last of his pursuers. He was tired of running and wanted this run to be finished. He gasped for more air, spotted a stack of lichen covered rock with a slight overhang, a scraggly bristlecone pine standing watch atop. With another look down the slope at his backtrail, Gabe slowly rose and made his way to his chosen, though temporary, refuge. He hunkered down behind the rock, scanning the crest of the ridge for all possible accesses, then turned to look behind him at the receding slope that would lead him to the small basin where he hoped to find Ebony and Wolf waiting.

The rattle of a rock turned him back to see the third warrior, slowly stretching up to peer over the crest, the predator stalking his prey. Gabe nocked an arrow as he hugged the rocks, watching the Blackfoot through a thin crack between the huge flat stones. The man cautiously rose higher, coming to his feet but still in a crouch, a bow with nocked arrow at his side, as he searched for any sign of Gabe, but the rocky crest was unyielding and held any evidence of the passing of a man in secret. No crushed plants, no turned stones, no footprints across the limestone rock, no blood trail, and the warrior scowled. He slowly scanned the rounded crest of the big round top mountain, looking for any obvious route his prey might have taken as he fled from his pursuers and carefully picked his steps as he moved, still in a crouch.

Gabe watched, waiting for the man to come into full view, the crest of the hilltop offered no cover, and the man would soon be exposed. Gabe did not want to rush his shot, remembering what happened with the other Blackfoot and he carefully brought the bow to full draw, lifting it as he readied his aim, knowing he would have to expose himself to take the shot, and slowly stepped away from the rock, but just as he was ready to release the arrow, he felt a sudden searing pain at his hip, causing him to flinch away as heard the clatter of a lance striking rock causing his arrow to fly askew. He glanced down at the shaft of the lance, noticed the broken point, and saw where it had sliced through the buckskin and cut his hip. He looked up to see the second warrior, leg showing dried blood, grabbing at a tomahawk at his belt and stumbling closer. Gabe spun away from the rock, snatching at the quiver for another arrow and nocking it as he saw the tomahawk tumbling through the air toward him.

Gabe threw himself to the side, the hawk flying past and clattering on the rocks. The arrow in his hand breaking as he fell. He looked up at the other warrior, charging toward him, screaming his war cry as he paused, brought his bow to full draw and loosed an arrow at Gabe. Already on the ground, Gabe rolled away, tumbling down the steep hillside and away from his pursuers. He grabbed at clumps of grass and anything in reach to break his fall, and drove his knee into the dirt, stopping his tumbling. But the last two arrows in the quiver were gone, the empty quiver hung loosely at his side.

A quick glance showed the two Blackfoot coming down the slope, digging in their heels, slipping, and sliding as they came. Gabe glanced down the slope, saw thicker trees and turned to flee. He ripped the string from the bow and tossed the useless weapon aside, felt at his waist for the knife and took to the trees. He ran, long strides taking him through the trees as he grabbed at one then another to keep from tumbling down the hillside. He moved at an angle across the steep slope, digging in his heels as he could, working his way closer to the little basin where his horse and Wolf waited.

The two warriors were falling back, the one with the wounded thigh slowing them down and Gabe heard them arguing, but he did not wait for the outcome. He lunged ahead, making short zig-zag cuts through the trees, sucking air as he ran, every muscle and bone protesting, but still he charged on, fleeing the two would-be killers. He heard something behind him, turned to take a quick glance over his shoulder, and as he did, his foot dropped between two broken limbs and he winced, tumbling to the ground, but catching himself with his hands. He rolled to the side, felt the grinding pain in his ankle and struggled to rise. He put his toe to the ground to test the ankle, the pain shooting up his leg, and he turned to face his pursuers.

He caught glimpses of the first one, dancing through the trees and heard the second one shouting from higher up the slope. Gabe stepped behind the nearest tree, looking for a club or something else he could use as a weapon, then felt at his hip for the knife, but it was gone. He shook his head, looking for anything to use against his pursuer, but there was nothing within reach and the man was coming quickly. Gabe's trail was easy to see, even in the deep shadows of the thick woods, he had made no attempt to obscure his trail, seeking only to put distance between him and the Blackfoot. He breathed deeply, feeling his heart beating like the war drum of the Salish, and searched both his surroundings and his mind, for something, anything.

The crashing of limbs and crunch of pine needles told of the nearness of the warrior and Gabe spun to his right, looking to his back trail, searching for the man, and once spotted, Gabe ducked behind another tree and worked his way back uphill, paralleling his original path. He moved only when he knew he was unseen, and stopped beside a big pine, hugging the rough bark and sap. The warrior was moving more stealthily, having lost sight of his quarry, choosing caution against such an adversary. He carried his bow with nocked arrow against his chest, picking his steps and glancing from the trail to the ground before him. Gabe was almost within reach, and slowly moved around the tree, keeping the big trunk between them. He favored his injured ankle, but had to force himself to ignore the pain, for he would have only one chance.

Gabe watched until the man lifted his back foot, shifting his weight to the downhill foot, and then glanced at his footing, watching each step. When his attention was on the trail before him and he was off balance with one foot lifted, Gabe lunged! He drove one hand to the left of the man's head, grabbing at the man's chin and jerking it swiftly to the side, with his other hand under the warrior's right arm, he wrenched the man's head to the side, snapping his neck. Both men fell forward, but Gabe extended his hand and caught himself as he landed atop the dead warrior. He rolled to the side, looked to the trees uphill searching for the other Blackfoot, but seeing nothing, he struggled erect, taking the warrior's bow and quiver, and snatching at his belt for the knife and tomahawk, just as an arrow whispered past his shoulder.

Gabe stepped behind the nearest tree, grabbing at

the quiver for an arrow. Gabe heard the Blackfoot crashing through the trees, screaming his war cry. As he fought to nock an arrow and turn to face his attacker, he heard a scream, different from a war cry, a scream of terror and a deep throated growl and snarl that was all too familiar. He stepped from behind the tree to see the black fur of Wolf and saw the big beast ripping at the throat to the Blackfoot, who was kicking and struggling, but just for a moment and then lay still, his body moved only by the big wolf that shook his head side to side as he straddled the body of the bloody warrior.

Gabe grinned and dropped to his knees, "Wolf! Wolf! Boy it's good to see you!" he declared as the wolf released his grip and turned a bloody maw to face Gabe. The face that was the terror of his victim, now opened in what Gabe saw as a smile, and the wolf turned and trotted toward his friend. Gabe reached out and hugged the bloody scruff and pulled Wolf close, running his hands through the thick fur and talking to his friend all the while laughing in relief.

Gabe looked at the two bodies, shook his head, and with Wolf helping, he rose to his feet and started through the trees, hobbling and limping, but determined to make it to Ebony. When he spotted the big black stallion, the horse lifted his head and nickered a greeting, then dropped his nose back to the grass he had been enjoying. Gabe went to Ebony's side, put his arms around his neck and hugged the big animal, stroking his neck, "And it's good to see you too, boy."

He untied his bedroll, rolled it out and picked up his spare set of buckskins, mumbling, "Guess I'm gonna hafta get Cougar Woman to make me another set," as he shook the britches out and laid them aside. He started stripping off the leggings and breach cloth taken from Kicking Horse and sat down in the grass to pull the britches on, favoring his ankle and other wounds when a voice came from behind him, "I cannot wait to hear how you lost your buckskins!" He recognized the voice of Cougar Woman, and turned to face her, trying to get to his feet, and stumbling as he moved. She sat her horse, smiling and laughing, as Ezra, Spotted Eagle, and Red Hawk grinned.

19 / AVENGE

As Gabe finished working at getting his rig on, Cougar tended to his wounds and the others stepped down and seated themselves to listen to Gabe's tale of the past two days. "So, when I guessed what they were doing, I had to warn the village of the Kutenai, but that didn't work out so well. I had to do something, so I figgered to stampede the horses, and then . . ." he continued to relate the events that brought him back to his horse in another man's clothes and the four sat back, laughing as he described running barefoot and naked through the trees.

Gabe winced as Cougar used strips of buckskin cut from the Blackfoot's leggings to bind up his ankle, but he knew it would be helpful as he tried to put his weight on the gimpy foot. Ezra pulled out some pemmican and shared it with Gabe and Cougar Woman as Spotted Eagle and Red Hawk worked at some smoked strips of venison. Gabe looked at Red Hawk, "I thought you'd be busy with your courtin'!"

Red Hawk grinned as he dropped his eyes to the ground, "A warrior must do as his war leader bids," he declared stoically, then glanced to his father to see him grinning.

Spotted Eagle explained, "He needed some time away to think clearly," as he fought to keep from laughing at his son. "The mother of the girls was mothering him, and he had to get away from her. She has taken over his lodge and he might never get it back." The others laughed, but the embarrassed Red Hawk just ducked his head and snatched at a long piece of grass to chew on to occupy himself. But it was the way of fathers and sons and close friends that were like family.

Spotted Eagle looked at Gabe, "What should be done about the Blackfoot?"

"Well, I reckon they'll stay camped through the night, prob'ly leave in the mornin'. They've got a good-sized herd of stolen horses, three captives, two women and a young man, that I saw, but any village or people that get in their way will be in trouble."

"How many warriors?"

"Uh, well, there's four less, and two others that guarded the herd, but near as I can figger, prob'ly three hands, or fifteen."

"And where is their camp?"

Gabe pointed to the round top mountain behind them, "On the other side of that ridge."

"They must be driven from this land or destroyed so they will not come again!" spat Spotted Eagle, standing and stomping to the trees.

Gabe glanced at Cougar and Ezra, then with a quick look to Red Hawk, "I don't think he's too happy with the Blackfoot, ya' reckon?"

They finished their pemmican and Gabe looked to Ezra, "I noticed you didn't bring a coffee pot and some coffee."

"Didn't figger to be gone that long."

"Since when did time have anything to do with your thirst for coffee?" asked Gabe, rising to go to the little spring for some water.

"Didn't wanna bring a pack horse, so . . ." suggested Ezra, following his friend.

Cougar walked beside Gabe her hand hooked in the crook of his arm. He looked at her and asked, "The young'uns?"

Cougar smiled, "Red Hawk's twins wanted to stay with Dove and help with them and we were both grateful. I needed to know you were alright."

Gabe grinned, dropped to one knee to scoop up some water in his hand, sipped at it and stepped aside so Cougar and Ezra could have their drink. When they walked back to the horses, Spotted Eagle had returned from his foray and sat beside his son, watching as the others returned. Gabe frowned as he dropped to his haunches before Eagle, "Looks like you've got a plan," he stated, noticing Eagle's intense expression with a furrowed brow over a staring glare.

Eagle grunted, motioning to the small patch of dirt before them, "Show me the camp."

Gabe knew he meant the camp of the Blackfoot and he picked up a stick and began to diagram what he remembered of the camp, as he drew he said, "You could climb that knob and look down on the camp, but I'm a little gimpy for that."

Eagle grunted again and listened as Gabe pointed out the upper clearing and meadow that held the herd, the line of trees that separated the camp of the warriors from the horses, and the thicker brush in the lower part of the valley near the mouth that opened to the lake. He stabbed at the camp, "The warriors were spread out here, here, and here. Their bedrolls near the trees. This part," pointing to the clearing below the camp, "is tall grass."

Spotted Eagle sat with legs crossed, his elbows on his knees, his chin in his hands as he stared at the dirt diagram. He reached out and pointed on either side, "Hills?"

"Yes," answered Gabe, then made a series of marks to show the hills, then pointed, "We are here," and then further, "the lake is here."

Eagle grunted again, looked up at the others and

began with a nod to Cougar, "You will come from here," pointing at the diagram, then nodded to Red Hawk, "you come from here and Black Buffalo will come from here." The areas he referenced were above and to the sides of the horse herd. He looked at Gabe, "You will be here," pointing to the lower part of the valley, just below the camp of the Blackfoot. "I will be the Dog Dancer, and as I return, you will begin." He explained further, making certain each one knew what their responsibility would be, then rose to his feet. "I go to prepare," and walked to his horse, untied his bedroll, and went to the edge of the trees.

Gabe frowned, looked at Cougar and Red Hawk, "What is a Dog Dancer?"

"I have only heard of it one time. It is the greatest deed of bravery of a warrior. I fear for my father."

Gabe scowled, looked to Cougar who shrugged her shoulders, unable to explain.

While Eagle prepared himself, Gabe and the others prepared their weapons, readying themselves for what they knew could be a very deadly fight. Although the plan of Spotted Eagle was similar to what Gabe had attempted, it would be more dangerous for it would be in the full light of day and the warriors would not be tired nor unwary. The most they could hope for was the surprise of the Blackfoot that anyone would attack them. But that arrogance could work to the advantage of Gabe and company.

Spotted Eagle had implied that Gabe would use his bow, so he uncased it and sat on the flat rock to string the Mongol bow. As he finished he looked up to see Spotted Eagle come from the trees, arrayed like Gabe had never seen. His long braids hung over each shoulder, framing the bone hair pipe breast plate. At his neck was a bone hair pipe choker, and silver discs the size of a twenty-dollar gold piece hung from his ears. A silver band encircled his upper right bicep, a beaded band at his left. A feathered fan sat behind his topknot, reminding Gabe of a strutting tom turkey. He held a coup stick, the size of a tall shepherd's crook, that was covered with strips of white fur, beaded bands, and scalp locks. He was an impressive and fearful warrior, his broad chest and oiled skin accented his muscular stature as he stood just over six feet and would top the scales at about fourteen stone, or one hundred ninety pounds. His stoic expression brokered no remarks as he lifted a red pipestone pipe and said, "I must prepare with the Spirits. You must pray with me."

Gabe lifted his eyebrows, glanced at the others, and nodded as Eagle came near. They sat in a circle and watched as Eagle stuffed tobacco in the pipe. Gabe had started a small hat size fire with dry grass and a handful of dry twigs that would emit little or no smoke. As Eagle nodded, Gabe lifted a firebrand to Eagle and watched as he lit the pipe. The man took a long draw, exhaled the smoke, then handed the pipe to Gabe who repeated the action, handing the pipe off to make the circle.

When Eagle accepted the pipe, he looked at Gabe, "We know the Son of God as Savior, and I ask you to pray for us before this fight. We go to save the captives and drive the Blackfoot from this place that is sacred to the memory of our people."

Gabe nodded, and joined hands with the others, and prayed, asking God to give them safety and wisdom, that the Blackfoot would leave, and the captives would be recovered. He added, "Lord, I'm not asking for anything different than what David needed as he went before Goliath, just for right to prevail over evil." He finished the prayer with an amen, then looked to Eagle, saw him sprinkle what looked like seeds in the bowl of the pipe atop the smoldering tobacco, then take a long draw, hold the smoke then slowly exhale. He repeated the action twice, then knocked the dottle out of the pipe, stood and nodded to the others. "You," motioning to Ezra, Cougar and Red Hawk, "must go now. Stay deep in the trees so you will not be seen. You will have two hands of sunlight to be in place." Gabe nodded, knowing that two hands represented the width of eight fingers, each representing fifteen minutes of time. He knew two hours would allow Red Hawk, who had the furthest to go, ample time to get in place.

Gabe watched as the three mounted up and stepped

beside Cougar. She leaned down, embraced her man and Gabe said, “Do not take unnecessary chances. You’re too important to me.”

“And you also, for you are important to me!” she declared, sitting upright, and reining her strawberry roan toward the trees. Gabe had explained to the three the lay of the land and the best route to take through the trees, and Red Hawk led off as they disappeared into the woods. He looked at Spotted Eagle, “The leader of this bunch is White Eagle, he is a wise leader, but he has my knives. I told him I would come back for them and he said if I did, he would give them to me, but I don’t think he thought I would come back.”

“Perhaps he will be wise and leave without a fight.”

Gabe shrugged, “Spotted Eagle, I think you and I both know that won’t happen. He is a Blackfoot and believes they are the most fearsome fighters of all. But as I remember things, we’ve tangled with ‘em a couple times and found that not to be so.”

“This is true. But this is the only time that matters.”

20 / DANCER

Spotted Eagle drew off to the side, obviously wanting to be alone. Gabe went to where Ebony was tethered, began checking his gear and glanced back at Eagle, saw him sitting, leaning against the trunk of a lone tree, eyes closed. Gabe frowned, not understanding what the man was doing and thought of the seeds or powder or whatever it was that Eagle put into the pipe bowl. He knew it was probably something that had been a practice of the Salish warriors, knowing there were many rituals that different peoples practiced on the advent of a battle, such as painting themselves and their horses, dancing themselves into a frenzy, seeking power from the spirits in many different ways. But he had never known Spotted Eagle to do any of those things, but he had not been around him prior to a battle such as they faced. He thought back to what the man mentioned that he would be the Dog Dancer and wondered, remembering that even Red Hawk did not fully understand, or at least did not explain, but did speak of his fear for his father.

Gabe glanced at the sun, thinking the time was near for them to start on their way. He glanced at Spotted Eagle, saw him rise and stretch, then look to Gabe and start his way. The horses were tethered near one another and Gabe turned to tighten the girth on his saddle, his back to Eagle. He heard Eagle as he mounted up and heard, "You lead until I say."

Gabe glanced his way, nodded, mounted up and gigged Ebony to the trail that led around the east end of the long ridge. He let Ebony have his head and felt him stretch out, glad to be back on the move. The trail quickly took them into the trees that were dense and towering, covering the shoulder of the round top mountains and blackened the ridge down the slope to water's edge. They came to a well-traveled trail that rounded the point and continued to the site of the Kutenai village at the point of the longer and higher ridge that pushed into the upper end of the lake, marking the northernmost shore. But they took a game trail that forked off and turned west into the mouth of the valley that held the Blackfoot camp. Gabe reined up and let Eagle come alongside, then spoke in soft tones, "The timber thins out and is a little sparse from here to the camp, but we could take to that slope yonder," nodding to the flank of the longer ridge, "and work our way up."

Eagle stood in his stirrups, looked at the scattered trees before them, then to the thicker timber on the slope of the ridge. He glanced at the sun, and turned to Gabe, "We go this way," he pointed to the timber to the right of the valley bottom, "we must be there soon." He looked back at Gabe, "I will lead."

Gabe slowly nodded, noticing a difference about the countenance of the man, but chose to wait and watch. Spotted Eagle was a proven warrior and war leader, there was nothing about the man that gave Gabe any misgivings or doubt, but he had grown curious. He let Eagle take the lead and followed close behind.

Red Hawk had taken the lead as the three left the camp, Cougar twisting in her saddle to look back at Gabe, then focused her attention forward. They took to the trees, moving up the valley but staying on the shoulder of the long ridge. Gabe had suggested taking the fourth cut that came from the ridge and as they dropped into the long gulch, a game trail offered a path over the ridge.

The trail wended its way through the thick timber, cutting the edge of a long aspen grove, and led them over a saddle that dropped them into the upper reaches of the valley with the Blackfoot. As they came to the lower end of the shoulder, they drew close and agreed to separate to go to the designated points above the clearing with the horses. Red Hawk led off, taking to the trees, and moving across the slight slope, watching the meadow below and working around the upper end of the clearing. Ezra was to go to the high point of the clearing, and Cougar stayed in the thick timber on the shoulder of the ridge to work her way to the south edge.

Cougar glanced to the sky for the position of the sun and guessed they were nearing their positions at about the right time, but from here on out, there was no certainty about what was to happen. As she kept to the trees, she saw a break in the timber that showed the clearing with the horse herd. Animals were scattered about, lazily grazing in the late afternoon sun. She saw two horses at the edge of the herd that were standing side by side, facing opposite directions and each one nibbling and scratching at the other's withers, but most others had heads down, noses in the tall grass. She stayed in the shadow of a tall ponderosa, searching for the two men that would be watching over the herd. A movement in the shadows caught her eye and she spotted first one, then the other further away, both keeping to the shade out of the bright high-country sun.

Cougar stepped down, loosely tethered her roan, and slowly moved closer, going from one tree to another when the warrior's head was turned, or his attention was on the horses. Her task was to silently take out this sentry, while Red Hawk took the other.

Ezra was to either begin the herd moving or move through the herd to the camp of the Blackfoot, but only after the sentries were down. And they were to wait until they knew the time was right, but Eagle had not told them exactly how they would know. Cougar found a big tree with a split trunk that offered cover and took her place to wait.

Spotted Eagle moved through the sparse cover, careful to keep trees before him and Gabe followed close behind. Within moments, they neared the edge of the trees, and Eagle reined up, holding an open palm low at his side to signal Gabe to stop. Eagle sat unmoving, waiting, then slowly turned to Gabe, motioned him down and Gabe slipped down from the saddle. He hung his quiver at his hip, held the Mongol bow in his left hand and moved alongside Eagle. Eagle bent low, whispering to Gabe, "I will go into the camp. As I near them, you send one of your screaming arrows over me to strike the ground before me." Gabe frowned, then looked around to see higher ground to his right.

"It would be better if I can take my shot from there," nodding to the shoulder that rose about fifty feet above the valley floor, bore heavy timber but had a clearing with a rock outcropping near the crest.

Eagle looked where he pointed, nodded, "Go."

Gabe quickly mounted Ebony, motioned Wolf before him and with the cover of the timber, soon made the clearing and lichen covered granite rocks. He left Ebony ground tied in the trees and went to the promontory, Wolf at his side, and saw Eagle below, and watched as the man pushed from the trees.

Eagle lifted his coup stick, resting the butt end near his knee and against the blanket that lay under his hide and wood saddle. He lifted his head to the sky and gigged the mount forward as he began chanting. Within moments, he was spotted by the Blackfoot who scampered for weapons, shouting at one another, but their leader, White Eagle, stepped forward with his arms uplifted, saying something to the men that Gabe could not hear. Gabe watched as Spotted Eagle neared the camp, noticed there were fewer warriors than he guessed, assuming the Kutenai had taken a toll when they were attacked. He saw Spotted Eagle rock his head back and took that as a signal. Gabe had nocked one of his whistler arrows and now lifted the bow, bringing it to full draw, and sent the arrow screaming overhead. Gabe watched, nocking another arrow, and saw the attention of the Blackfoot turn to the strange phenomenon that screamed high above and toward them. He saw the warriors moving, pointing high, and chattering to one another. The arrow arced high, then bent toward the ground, impaled in the grass almost at the feet of White Eagle. Some of the Blackfoot pointed to the arrow, then turned to search for the shooter, but there was no one within what they believed was the range of a bow. Then they looked at the mounted warrior approaching them and Gabe watched, mesmerized, as Spotted Eagle, still chanting and wailing, rode directly toward the Blackfoot camp. As he neared, the warriors, following the example of their leader, parted, moving to each side, watching the Salish war leadcr, slowly ride between them, still chanting, eyes heavenward, paying no attention to the Blackfoot.

What Gabe was watching was the Dog Dancer, seemingly in a trance, and as he thought of it, probably from the seeds added to the tobacco, riding into and through the camp of the enemy, untouched and unhindered. Spotted Eagle rode between the two groups of Blackfoot who stood staring, several wanting to strike the man, but were stayed by their leader who stood with arms raised, watching the man pass.

White Eagle recognized the man as a leader and high-ranking warrior, his attire, headdress, and the scalps on his coup stick spoke of his standing. But White Eagle had never seen such a display of bravery and courage, and then considered if it was something more. He frowned, looking around to find the shooter, saw nothing then stepped forward and plucked the arrow from the ground. He looked at the long black shaft, scowled, because it was unlike any arrow he had seen, the point was metal, the feathers black, and it was longer than any others. Most arrows would have identifying marks or makings that would identify the tribe and often the individual warrior, but there was nothing familiar about this arrow. He fingered the long hollow bone, recognizing that as the source of the scream or whistle, grinned and shook his head. White Eagle looked to the Salish warrior, saw him move through the trees toward the horses and motioned two warriors to follow, but before they made the trees, the Salish warrior reined around to ride back through the camp.

When Spotted Eagle broke from the trees into the clearing with the horse herd, he lifted his voice in the wailing chant as a signal to his people, then reined around and started back. Cougar Woman and Red Hawk recognized Spotted Eagle and knew that was the signal. Almost simultaneously, they sent arrows to pierce the chest of the two sentries and watched them fall to the ground, dead.

Gabe's promontory was about a hundred fifty yards from the camp of the Blackfoot, and he watched the warriors carefully. He lifted his brass telescope, shielding it from the sun, and made a quick scan of the warriors, watching their interaction with their leader, White Eagle. Gabe focused on White Eagle, stretched out the scope, and grinned as he recognized his knives hanging on the lanyard from Eagle's neck. He replaced the scope in its case at his belt, lifted his bow and watched as Spotted Eagle came back into the upper end of the camp. Gabe heard the wail and chant, heard it lift in volume then suddenly stop. Gabe frowned and leaned forward, watching. He heard Spotted Eagle speak loudly in the Blackfoot tongue but in a monotone that sounded as if he was in a trance. "I am Spotted Eagle of the Salish people. I speak to White Eagle, war leader of the Blackfoot. You and your warriors must leave this valley, without your captives and stolen horses, or you will all die. You will be killed by the great warrior, Spirit Bear and the black warrior known as Black Buffalo, who will ride among you and will kill you with his horn! So it is said, so it shall be!" Spotted Eagle had kept his eyes on the heavens, appearing as in a trance and never looked at the Blackfoot. When he fell silent, he gigged his horse forward and moved among them. Gabe saw a warrior at the edge of the group raise a lance, readying his throw at the Dog Dancer, and Gabe quickly sent an arrow, taking the man in the side under his uplifted arm, driving him to the ground. Gabe nocked another arrow, searching for another target of necessity. Several that stood near the downed man, shouted, causing the others to come near, followed by White Eagle. He looked at the arrow, then turned to look in the direction for the shooter, but Gabe had stepped behind a tree, still watching, but under cover.

The thunder of many hooves turned everyone's attention to the trees, knowing the herd was stampeding and would come crashing through the timber. Gabe went to Ebony, swung aboard, and hung the quiver at the cantle, the bow from the saddle horn, and wheeled Ebony around to take the trail through the trees to meet Spotted Eagle at the tree line. At the rumble of the herd, both men moved to the edge of the trees on the north side of the camp, watching the scampering and running Blackfoot as they sought cover from the stampede. Gabe saw two warriors snatch up blankets to try to turn the herd, but to no avail and he shook his head as they dove into the brush away from the herd.

As the last of the horses began to clear the trees, Gabe heard the war cry and scream of Ezra and watched as he charged through the trees, war club at the ready and at the first sight of a warrior, brought the heavy club arching overhead and split the skull of the man. Gabe dug heels to Ebony and charged into the melee, snatching up the two saddle pistols and earing back the hammers. Ebony shouldered through the nearest bunch and Gabe let loose with both pistols. The big pistols bucked and roared, spitting lead death, and dropped one man on either side of the big black, Gabe cocked the second hammers and blasted two more, parting the tide of flesh to drive closer to the club wielding Ezra.

Ezra was making a roundhouse swing with the ironwood death stick, and flattened two warriors, one head splitting and splattering brain matter and blood all about. The other doing a backward somersault to landing crosswise on his broken neck and caved in head. Gabe heard the war cry of Red Hawk, saw him, lance held low, charge a warrior that struggled to nock an arrow, but the lance drove him to the ground and the arrow fluttering harmlessly away. Without slowing his mount, Red Hawk pulled the lance free, swung it back to the fore and charged at another.

Gabe jammed the pistols in their holsters, snatched his Bailes over/under pistol from his belt and with one smooth motion, eared back the hammer and dropped it on the swing, the bullet blossoming blood at the base of the neck of a Blackfoot. Gabe swiveled the barrels, cocked the second hammer, and looked to see a warrior bringing his bow to bear on the charging Cougar Woman, guiding her roan with her legs, her bow at full draw and before Gabe could fire, Cougar's arrow buried itself in the chest of the one who had his arrow coming to bear on her. But the feathers of the fletching on Cougar Woman's arrow fluttered at the man's chest as he looked down, knowing he was dead even before he fell to his back, eyes staring at the sky.

Gabe nodded to his woman, saw another taking aim and brought his pistol to bear, discharging the lead missile and burying it in the man's forehead, his stare going cross-eyed as he stiffened and fell back like a dead tree falling in the forest. Gabe jammed the pistol home behind his belt and lifted the bow, nocking an arrow and looking for a target. He saw Cougar take down another with her arrow, saw Spotted Eagle charging into the camp, his arrows flying as he guided his war horse with his knees. Gabe turned, looking for Ezra, and saw his back as he drove his mount through the last of the Blackfoot, swinging his war club, once arc to the right, one to the left, each time laying a warrior down, dead and bleeding.

And suddenly, it was quiet. The five mounted warriors, turning, looking, watching. Gabe saw Ezra turn his mount and start back toward his friend, looking at the strewn bodies, holding his war club across his chest, ready to wield it again if necessary, but nothing moved. A moan came from one prone figure, a knee raised, then dropped, and silence. The only sound, the steps of Ezra's big bay, picking his way among the bodies and debris, to stop beside his friend. Both men were bloody, Ezra more so, and they looked with empty eyes to one another. Cougar Woman pushed her mount close beside Gabe's and reached out to touch her man's arm and leaned over to put her forehead on his shoulder and placed her hand on his chest, feeling his heart pounding like hers as they sat together, relieved and recovering.

Red Hawk and Spotted Eagle sat beside one another, heads down, breathing heavy as they rested. Spotted Eagle looked at Gabe and company, then looked around the camp. He saw the two Kutenai women, bound together, and tied to a tree, both looking wide eyed at the five warriors before them. Gabe spotted the young man, tied to another tree away from the women, and motioned to Red Hawk to free all of them. Gabe searched for White Eagle, saw his form near another, and stepped down. He walked to the side of the war leader, saw his eyes flutter, and reached out to cut the lanyard and retrieve the knives. White Eagle's hand grasped Gabe's, then lifted his eyes to the white man, whispered, "I said I would give them to you." He let out a raspy breath, dropped his hand, and sightless eyes stared at the blue sky.

21 / KTUNAXA

With a sweep of his hand, Spotted Eagle motioned the others to follow him from the camp of the Blackfoot. He turned toward the mouth of the valley, the sun at their backs. When they put the scattered timber and the flat of the valley behind them, they came to the trail that led north to the point and the site of the Kutenai village. Ezra and Red Hawk had caught three mounts for the captives and they followed the others, with Ezra bringing up the rear. When they turned on the trail, Spotted Eagle stopped and twisted around to summon the three Ktunaxa to his side and called for Cougar Woman to join them. He looked at them, began to speak in Salish and some sign, but looked to Cougar to translate. She watched and listened, then turned to the three, "We will go to your village, look for sign of any that escaped, do what we can for the dead."

The older woman pushed past the others, spoke directly to Cougar Woman, "There were some that left before the attack. We," nodding to the others, "and more, stayed to try to defend the village, but they came too fast. The leaders left most of the horse herd. They hoped the Blackfoot would take the animals and leave."

Spotted Eagle listened as Cougar translated, nodded, then asked, "Those that stayed, warriors?"

"Most, but not all. Some went with the others to protect them if the Blackfoot pursued."

Spotted Eagle understood the tactic and knew it would have been a hard decision for the leaders to make, but if they all fled, the Blackfoot would pursue and catch them without cover and kill them all, but by splitting their number, perhaps some would escape. Eagle nodded, turned away and started up the trail.

It was another scene of desolation and vengeful destruction. Mutilated bodies were scattered about, scavengers fought and tore at the carcasses, the smell of smoke, burned flesh, and death filled the air as a hush fell on the group. The horses picked their way among the debris and tears cut a trail down the cheeks of dust covered faces, each with stoic and angry expressions. One of the women jumped down and ran at a band of turkey buzzards picking at a carcass, waving her arms, and screaming to drive the carrion eaters away. She dropped to her knees, reached out to touch the body, but was repulsed by the blood and gore and smell. She buried her face in her hands, her shoulders shaking as she wept. The other Ktunaxa woman slipped from her mount and went to the side of her friend, dropped to one knee beside her and put an arm around her shoulders, pulling her close.

Gabe sidled up to Spotted Eagle and asked, "What do we do?"

Eagle looked at his friend, glanced at Ezra and Cougar, and said, "They," motioning to the bodies, "must be respected."

Gabe nodded, looking around and walked Ebony to a tall steep butte with a shear talus slope facing the ruins of the village. He turned away and returned to the others, "We'll take the bodies there," pointing to the bluff, "we can cave that ledge off to cover the bodies."

Ezra and Cougar nodded, and everyone stepped down, dug out the hemp ropes and braided rawhide ropes from their bedrolls and saddle bags and started the gruesome task of gathering the bodies. The young man of the Ktunaxa, Black Badger, joined the others in the work while the women, Buffalo Tail and Bear Killer, sorted through the remnants of the village for anything worth salvaging.

The sun dipped behind the western mountains, leaving the reminder of a golden sky, when Spotted Eagle stopped the work, although little had been done and said, "Let us go from here, find a place that smells good and have a meal and rest. We will do more when light comes."

No one argued, and all quickly mounted to follow Eagle as he took to the trail and moved around the bend and point of the ridge to a small clearing at water's edge. Everyone pitched in with the needed tasks to make their camp, Gabe and Ezra tended the horses, Red Hawk and Black Badger gathering the firewood and the women assembling the makings of a meal. When Cougar saw the meager pile of pemmican and smoked meat, she shook her head and went to Gabe's side, "There is little enough to eat. Would you try to find a deer or something?"

Gabe's eyebrows lifted as he turned to look at the beginnings of dusk, then smiled at his woman, "I'll do what I can."

She turned to Ezra, "There is a stream that comes into the lake there," nodding down the shore, "you could get some fish."

Ezra grinned, nodded, "Yes ma'am!" he declared, grinning, and going to his gear for some fishing tackle.

Cougar returned to the women and suggested they all disperse and find other edibles and return soon. Everyone nodded, smiling, and scattered in different directions. Spotted Eagle, Red Hawk and Black Badger watched as the others left and Eagle set the example by going to the water to wash off some of the stench of death which the two younger warriors followed. As they came from the water, they were stopped when they saw a group standing near the trees at the edge of the clearing. Black Badger shouted and ran forward, greeting the leader and speaking rapidly. He gesticulated toward Spotted Eagle and Red Hawk, motioned to the makings of a camp fire and the tethered horses, obviously explaining to the group about those that rescued him and the two women.

Spotted Eagle and Red Hawk dried off with a blanket as they watched the others, knowing they were returnees from the Kutenai village and when the initial chattering receded, Black Badger led a man with a touch of grey in his hair, to Spotted Eagle. Using sign, he introduced the leader of the village, Crazy Owl.

Although sign language was an effective way of communicating between those of different tongues, it lacked in many ways including making the thoughts and concerns clearly understood. When speaking of things and events is one thing, but describing opinions and interests requires the spoken language. The consternation between the two leaders was evident and when Spotted Eagle saw Cougar Woman returning, he waved her over.

Spotted Eagle spoke to Cougar Woman, "This is Crazy Owl of the Ktunaxa. He is the leader of the village. He asks why we are here. Would you tell him?"

Cougar Woman nodded and began, using both sign and her limited knowledge of the Ktunaxa tongue, but she was quickly learning with her recent conversations with the refugees that took shelter with the Salish. She spoke at length with Crazy Owl, telling of the attack against the Salish, the lower village of the Ktunaxa, and the actions of Spirit Bear. When she mentioned Spirit Bear, the leader showed recognition and immediately asked, "You are a friend of Spirit Bear?"

"He is my mate," answered Cougar, frowning. "How do you know him?"

"He brought warning to our people. If he had not come, we would have all been killed. He said he would do what he could to stop the attack, but the Blackfoot still came against the village. Does Spirit Bear still live?"

Cougar smiled, nodding, "Yes, he has gone to get meat for us. He will return soon."

Just the mention of the man who had come to warn the people had dropped the barriers between them. Crazy Owl turned to the five warriors behind him, sent two away and turned back to Cougar Woman. "We are grateful for what you have done. The Salish have always been friends of the Ktunaxa, and we stand with them against the Blackfoot."

Spotted Eagle nodded as Cougar gave the translation, "We will help you with the dead," nodding toward the village, "and with the horses. There are many that will be returned to the Ktunaxa that have come to our village. We will tell them of your village if they want to join with you."

Crazy Owl nodded, "Who is the leader of that village?"

"I do not know. All the men of the village were killed. Only the women and children escaped in the canoes and came to our village. The Blackfoot had attacked our village, but were turned away, most were killed."

The chief looked around at the camp and horses, frowned, and looked back at Spotted Eagle, "Where are your warriors?"

Spotted Eagle grinned, "Spirit Bear and Black Buffalo are hunting for meat and will return soon. My son," nodding toward Red Hawk, "and Spirit Bear's woman, Cougar Woman, are the only warriors."

"You lost many?"

"No, we lost no one."

The chief frowned, looked at Eagle, then at Red Hawk and Cougar Woman, counted on his fingers and asked, "You went against the Blackfoot with one hand of warriors? And killed them all?"

"Yes."

The man's eyes flared, and he looked to his warriors to see if they heard and understood. He turned back to Spotted Eagle, "I have never known of such great warriors as the Salish."

Spotted Eagle answered, "You met Spirit Bear, his friend Black Buffalo and his woman," nodding to Cougar Woman, "are not Salish, but are friends with the Salish and the Ktunaxa. And I think my son," nodding to Red Hawk and chuckling, "will take one of the Ktunaxa for his woman."

Crazy Owl glanced from Eagle to Red Hawk and back, saw the amused expression on Spotted Eagle and nodded, "It is a good thing for our people to be joined."

As they spoke, Black Buffalo returned with a long willow forked stick that held several sizable trout, but he paused as he saw the visitors, looked down at the fish, and shook his head, knowing there were not enough for so many, but he heard Gabe approaching and looked to see him with the carcass of a mule deer across his shoulders. He chuckled and said, "Sure glad you got one! Looks like we got comp'ny for dinner!"

22 / RETURN

First light brought considerable activity to the north-west shore of the great Salish Lake. The surviving Kutenai returned to the site of their village and took over the task of tending to the burial of the villagers, while Gabe and company, with the help of several of the Ktunaxa, started the round up of the horse herd. With the combined herd from the two villages, there were about a hundred fifty horses to gather, but most had lingered in the mouth of the valley where the grass was deep and water nearby. Since all the horses were used to people and had been handled and used, they responded to the gatherers and by mid-day, the herd was milling about in the mouth of the valley. The Ktunaxa set about sorting out the animals of the upper village, and within the hour, Gabe and company had the herd on the move to the south.

With Red Hawk taking the point, Ezra and Spotted

Eagle riding flank, and Gabe and Cougar Woman taking drag, they started the herd along the trail that hugged the west shore of the lake. With the shoreline and water keeping the horses together on the left, Spotted Eagle and Ezra kept them from taking to the trees on the right, Gabe and Cougar Woman kept them moving. Red Hawk rode before the herd, giving the animals one to follow and they pushed onward. The horses had grown lazy with the last few days grazing in the upper meadow and most seemed to readily move with the herd.

The day started with a clear sky, cool breezes, and mild temperatures, but Gabe had been watching the clouds that were moving in from the northeast, kicking up the wind and dropping the temperature. He knew they would spend another night on the trail, probably reaching the village by late afternoon on the next day, and he was not concerned about the weather. Yet his experience in the mountains had taught him to take nothing for granted and to be ready for anything. They were not in the high mountains, the granite tipped peaks that stood above timberline, but they were high enough to get some deadly mountain storms. As the temperature dropped, the drovers had turned up collars, hunkered into their robes or jackets, and pushed closer to the herd, appreciative of the combined body heat of the moving animals.

The sun was dropping behind the mountains in the

west when Red Hawk turned in the trail and waved the herd into a bit of a basin with tall grass for the night's stay. The riders held back, letting the horses settle down and start to graze. Red Hawk motioned to an area around a point of timber that he selected for their camp and everyone readily rode into the break of the trees and the clearing that sided a small stream that cut through the bigger meadow on its way to empty into the lake.

While the others tended the animals and circled the herd to settle them down, Gabe and Cougar Woman readied the meal. Cougar had kept the back straps of the deer wrapped in a piece of the hide and brought them out to cut into steaks for broiling over the fire. She had a bundle of camas bulbs and readied them for the coals. Gabe cut the steaks, fetched some willows to hang the steaks and once the fire was going with hot coals, he hung the meat over the fire. Cougar stuffed the camas roots in the edge of the coals, and the two sat back to enjoy a few moments of quiet together.

Wolf lay beside them, and pushed closer on one side, Cougar on the other. Gabe put his arm around Cougar and drew her close, prompting her to snuggle against him, "You feel nice and warm," she mumbled, "it's getting cool for this time of year."

"I'm thinkin' there might be a storm rollin' in, been watchin' the clouds back thataway," nodding to the northeast.

"I saw them. They have dark bellies."

Gabe grunted, knowing clouds with dark undersides often brought storms, but this time of year the most he expected was a good rainstorm that would bring much needed moisture. Although the north country where they were was not as dry as their home country further south, it had been too long since they had a good rain and the grass was starting to brown. They were hopeful of a good rain, and Gabe knew they would need to slap together some lean-tos for some protection in case it came in the night.

The others soon returned to camp and Ezra reported, "They're settled down, I don't think they'll be goin' anywhere tonight."

Spotted Eagle nodded his agreement, "They are content with the good grass and water close by, the drive has made them happy for the rest."

Gabe turned to Spotted Eagle, "You think that storm," nodding to the rolling clouds he had been watching, "will spook 'em any?"

Eagle looked at the gathering clouds, shaking his head slowly, "They are used to storms, they will move close together and turn their tails to the wind to wait it out."

"And we better get busy with a lean to, unless we wanna lay in a puddle all night!" declared Ezra, starting to the trees to start collecting branches and more. Fortunately, there was a wide growth of lodgepole pine on the north facing slope of the hill behind their camp and Ezra enjoined Red Hawk to help as they cut several of the tall skinny trees for their lean to. Using the trees at the edge of the clearing, they spanned the space between three, using the long poles for the cross brace to make two adjoining shelters. Other poles were laid from the ground to the cross beam and covered first with ground cover hides taken from the Blackfoot camp, then overlaid with the branches, laying them with the stump end on the high end, utilizing the needles to help shed the water. A pair of buffalo robes and several blankets, used by the Blackfoot as riding blankets, were used as ground cover upon which they spread their bedrolls. It was more than what was usually done for one night on the trail, but with the probability of a storm, they opted for comfort and warmth.

The shelters were on the high ground near the flank of the taller of the hills, but purposely chosen to be away from any runoff. The nearby timber would give a wind break and their horses would be tethered in the trees on the lee side of the shelters. Ezra stood and looked at the finished sanctuaries and satisfied, glanced to Spotted Eagle and Red Hawk for their affirmation, and the three walked back to the fire for some supper.

Ezra looked at Gabe, "The little one's," nodding toward the lean tos, "for Cougar Woman and Wolf, but if they'll let'chu, you might crowd in amongst 'em. Us men'll need all the room in the big'un."

Gabe snickered at Ezra, "And this hyar meat's for us'ns. But if you cuddle up to Wolf, he might share his with you!"

Ezra sat near Gabe, looked at the sizzling steaks hanging over the fire, glanced around and asked, "Where's the coffee?"

"Uh, you left it with Dove, remember?"

"Oh yeah. Hope she 'preciates it! It's quite a sacrifice for me to make, I hope you know."

"Ummhmm, it would sure taste good on a night like this," proclaimed Gabe, looking at the stars. He turned to look to the northeast and saw a black sky, clouds hiding the stars and a cool breeze whistled across the treetops. "Dunno 'bout that storm. Don't see no lightnin' yet, but . . ."

"Yeah, but!" answered Ezra, "We both know what can come after that 'but!' But," he paused, grinning, "we made some fine shelters over there, so even if it does come a blusterin' an' bangin' our way, I think we'll be comf't'ble."

Cougar Woman looked at Gabe, nodded, and Gabe said, "Let's ask the Lord's blessing, shall we?" and doffed his hat to pray. When he finished, he donned his hat and reached for one of the willow withes that held a sizzling steak and brought it close. He took a bite of the juicy meat, then used the end of the stick to drag a camas root within reach. They had not packed for the extended trip and had to make do without plates and such, but the lack of utensils proved to be little hindrance for the hungry travelers.

Scraps were tossed to Wolf and quickly disappeared, until a long howl rose from back in the hills, trailed off with a couple of barks, and Wolf came to his feet, looking in the direction of the mournful cry. Another howl lifted into the darkness and Wolf trotted to the edge of the clearing and answered. No one spoke, and all watched the big black beast as he responded to the call of the wild.

Wolf turned to look back at those around the campfire, saw the slight nod from Gabe, and launched himself into the blackness of the night. The howls came again and again, Gabe recognizing the answering call of Wolf as he pursued the singer in the solitude and turned back to the others. "Hope he comes back 'fore the storm hits, or maybe that his girlfriend has a warm, dry cave for his romantic interlude."

Red Hawk frowned, "Interlude?"

"You know, his little time with the she-wolf."

Red Hawk lifted his head slightly in a slow nod and glanced at his father. But Spotted Eagle had nothing to add to the brief conversation and sat stoically silent.

As the fire faded, the cool breeze encouraged everyone to go to the shelter and crawl into the blankets, but Gabe was restless and told Cougar, "I'm gonna look around a bit."

Cougar nodded, knowing the moods and concerns of her man, believing he was thinking about Wolf as well as the horses. She scurried under the blankets and smiled as she watched him walk around the point of trees to look at the lake in the waning moonlight. Gabe stood before the break in the trees that led to the trail and the lake beyond. Where he stood was high enough to enable him to look over the treetops along the shore and see the water. On a still night, the surface of the lake would reflect the stars and the light of the moon, but rolling waves tossed back shards of broken light as if sending a coded message of turmoil. Yet Gabe saw an uncertain beauty in the sparkling surface that continually moved with the energy of the coming storm. He looked to the storm clouds and saw the flash of lightning deep within, giving a luminescence to the clouds, a muted light that hung in the heavens. The low rumble of distant thunder was lower than the growl of Wolf but menacing none the less. He shook his head as he turned back to the clearing, hoping to see his furry friend, but saw only the low glow of coals of the cookfire.

23 / BEDLAM

Gabe stepped back through the line of trees, and keeping the tree line at his back, walked between the herd and the smaller clearing that held the camp and shelters. He stopped as he heard another howl from a wolf, but closer than before. It was quickly answered by another, seeming to come from the flat above the basin that held the horses. Gabe's hackles rose, and he trotted to the shelter to retrieve his rifle. He kicked Ezra's foot, hissed, "Get your rifle and come with me!"

Ezra rolled from his blankets, came to his knees, and crawled out of the shelter, rifle in hand. He reached back for his hat, then asked Gabe, "What's goin' on?"

"I think the wolf pack is coming for the horses!"

Red Hawk stuck his head from the lean to, "Shall we come?"

Gabe whispered his reply, "No, just some wolves. We can handle it!"

"This way!" he whispered to Ezra and trotted into the trees. Gabe led them just over a hundred yards, staying in the thick trees but following the edge of the meadow that lay in the basin with the horses. His glance showed the horses, no longer standing hipshot and dozing, but with heads up and looking to the trees and the hills beyond. Gabe stopped, pointing to the trees that bordered the uphill side of the basin, "I think the pack is coming from higher up and are in those trees yonder. You hang out near here; I'll go toward the other end." He started to caution Ezra against shooting any black wolf, but knew his friend needed no reminder, and started through the trees.

As he trotted through the timber, a glance to his left showed a moonlit meadow, smaller than the one with the horses, but open, grass waving in the breeze. As he moved, he tried to think what the wolves would do, *Prob'ly stay in the trees till they get near, avoid the open grass.* He felt the breeze on his face, frowned, knowing the breeze would carry his scent across the meadow, but that could work to his advantage. They weren't out to kill the wolf pack, just protect the horses, and if his scent turned the pack away, all the better.

But the churning of the storm clouds shifted the wind. It had been coming along the flanks of the mountains, moving the north/south length of the lake, but when it shifted, the wind tumbled from the higher mountains, bringing colder air, and blowing from the back of the pack toward the horse herd. When Gabe felt the change, he looked at the horses, saw heads come up, ears pricked and many getting skittish. Several started backing away from the tree line, looking over their shoulder at the break in the trees that led to the trail and the lake. Gabe searched the trees at the upper end, watching for any movement. He brought his rifle to his shoulder, bringing it to full cock as he did, knowing the dim light would obscure his sights, but he had made many instinctive shots before and would again.

He glanced from the trees to the horses and back again, judging the unseen approach of the wolves by the movement of the horses, and he rested his finger lightly on the forward trigger, waiting. And from the dark shadows of the timber, slinked a stalking wolf, stretched out, belly gliding over the tips of the grass. He was close enough for Gabe to see the snarl of his muzzle, the orange of his eyes, and the long teeth that dripped drool. He let the wolf move a little closer, making sure of his shot, and squeezed the trigger.

Orange flame stabbed the night, the blast of the flintlock echoing back from the hillside, to be answered by another roar from the far side of the meadow. Gabe dropped the butt of the rifle to his hip, spun the trigger guard to open the breech and drove the patched ball home. He dumped the powder into the breech, capped the horn, and spun the trigger guard back to close the breech. He used his smaller horn to prime the lock, dropped the frizzen and lifted the rifle to his shoulder. All the movements of loading were done by touch, Gabe's eyes searching the trees and grass for another wolf. With the rifle at his shoulder, muzzle down, he looked from the trees to the horses, noted the horses were still skittish, moving back, some trotting to the break in the trees, and Gabe slowly moved across the top of the meadow, speaking softly to the horses, but watching for more of the pack.

He was startled by another shot from Ezra, and frowned, knowing that was from a pistol and not the big Lancaster rifle. He kept moving in that direction, knowing the horses could easily see him and would probably be reassured by the presence of a man they knew to be friendly. Gabe also knew the horses had been used for hunting and in battle and the sound of gunfire was not strange nor frightening to them, but the presence of wolves always spelled trouble, although most of the animals had seen the black wolf that stayed with the man, the distinct smell of a wolf in the wild was different than one that had the smell of man about him.

When Gabe had moved away to go to the trees above the meadow, Ezra found a point of rocks that suited him for a place to watch for the wolves. It would give him some cover, break up his outline for any animal looking his way, and offer a place to sit while he waited. He dropped to a flat rock, lay his rifle across his knees, and searched the trees and the upper meadow for any movement other than the horses. He felt his hackles rise and slowly stood, searching the shadows, the dim light of the moon offering little help. He looked at the horses, saw several with uplifted heads and ears pricked, and he turned his attention back to the tree line.

He knew Gabe had time to get to the far side and was probably watching the trees as well. Ezra looked that direction, trying to determine where Gabe would be, marking the probable points in his mind to ensure he would not shoot that direction. As he swung his eyes back along the trees, he froze. Standing no more than thirty feet before him was a big grey wolf, he guessed a she-wolf, who stood staring at the herd. She turned to look toward Gabe, and Ezra slowly brought his rifle to his shoulder, lifting the muzzle for a shot just as she turned back toward the herd. She slowly lowered to a stalking stance, one forefoot lifted, head down, lip curling and teeth showing. As she stretched one foot forward, a rifle shot came from across the flat, but the she-wolf was ready to lift the second foot to start her stalk, the Lancaster roared and spat an orange lance that sent the shadow of death to bust her shoulder and drive her to the ground.

Ezra dropped the butt of the rifle beside his foot,

grabbing for a ball and patch in his possibles bag, brought it up and seated it in the muzzle, slapped it into the muzzle with the heel of his hand, and grabbed for the ram rod. As he slipped it from the ferrules, a growl behind him stopped his movement. He dropped the ram rod, snatched at his pistol, and cocked it as he spun to face the new threat. He dropped the hammer as grey fur blocked his vision of the moon. The pistol roared and flame showed the fur of the chest of the big wolf, just as the paws struck Ezra's chest. But the big man spun away, the teeth of the wolf barely missing his face, and he slapped the beast aside. Ezra grabbed at his knife, brought it up and he leaped onto the twisting and turning wolf. But before the beast could move, almost two hundred pounds of riled muscle slammed on its chest, driving the wind from his lungs, breaking his ribs, and the razor-sharp blade of the knife stabbed at the beast's throat. The blade rose and fell again and again, Ezra growling and grunting as he bared his own teeth and smashed at the head and mouth of the grey wolf until the beast moved no more.

Ezra gasped for air, his shoulders lifting, and he looked around, searching for any other wolves of the pack. The horses had moved to the lower end of the meadow, nearer the break in the trees, but it appeared none had gone to the trail. Ezra stood, sheathed his knife, and picked up his rifle and ramrod. He drove the ball home, replaced the ram rod, and primed the pan, slapping the frizzen down. He leaned back against the rock pile and looked toward the upper end, searching for Gabe. He saw the shadowy figure of his friend moving through the knee-deep grass and waited.

As Gabe neared, he spoke softly, "I think the rest took off." He stepped from the grass, came closer and paused as he saw the carcass of the wolf. He looked up at Ezra, "The second shot?"

"And more," answered Ezra. "The first 'un was there," nodding behind Gabe toward the edge of the trees, "but this'n came from this pile of rocks," pointing with his chin as he turned, "had to finish him with my knife."

Gabe saw the dark spots on Ezra's buckskins, understanding. "Didn't see no black'uns, thankfully," added Ezra as they turned to go back to camp.

Ezra lay his rifle over his shoulder, glanced to the sky, "I reckon that storm's shapin' up to be a tree shaker!"

Gabe looked heaven ward, "Ummhmm, believe so."

They had taken but another step and raindrops began to pelt them, prompting them to trot the rest of the way back to the shelters. Red Hawk and Spotted Eagle stood in the dark shadows of the pine and stepped forward as Gabe and Ezra came back into camp. Eagle asked, "Blackfoot?"

"Nah, just a pack of wolves, hungry an' huntin'," answered Gabe, stepping close to the shelters. Both men knew Eagle and Hawk would have come to their aid, but to approach a fight in the darkness could endanger both friend and foe.

The men crawled into the sanctuaries, laying their rifles beside them, and slipped under their blankets. Cougar rolled to her side to greet her man, "Is it not late for hunting?"

"Not for wolves!" declared Gabe and pulled her close.

As he looked at his woman, he was surprised to see the big black wolf lying on the other side of her and looking at him as if he were asking the same question. Gabe looked from Wolf to Cougar Woman, "He been here all the time?"

"Ummhmm, came back right after you left."

Gabe shook his head, lay back and Cougar rested her head on his chest, "I like the rain," she declared.

"I think this is gonna be more'n rain."

24 / DELUGE

The steady patter of raindrops on the cover was soothing and lulled most to sleep, but Gabe was still concerned, not liking the looks of the thunderheads that appeared to be coming their way. As he lay listening to the rain, he reviewed their preparations and believed they had done all they could, but still he grew restless. He sat up, leaning to the opening to look out in the stormy darkness.

As he looked to the north, he saw a bolt of naked white lightning drive its crooked lance into the ground, then counted the seconds until he heard the growl of thunder. *What we're gettin' now is just a teaser of what's comin'. The worst of it is still 'bout three, four miles away and takin' its time gettin' here.* He shook his head as he sat with elbows crooked around his uplifted knees. He muttered a short prayer for safety, but knew they were going to get hit, and hit hard. *No sense wakin' the others, they'll come awake soon 'nuff.* He glanced over his shoulder at Cougar Woman, sound asleep with a smile on her face, and Wolf, stretched out with his face between his paws, but as Gabe watched, he saw Wolf was also restless.

He glanced to his left, saw the little stream, that came from the hilltop and a couple springs that fed it, was now more than the trickle it had been. Wherc before all it took was a stretch and a step to cross, it was now starting to crash through the trees, carrying storm debris in its four-foot-wide flood waters. The shelters had been erected on high ground, and for now, were out of reach of the rising creek, however rivulets of water were coursing down the hillside and laying the grass low as they pushed toward lower levels.

He thought of their gear, stacked under a big ponderosa, covered with hides and blankets and with branches and rocks weighting things down keep them sheltered. Most of his weapons Gabe had handy, his rifle, both saddle pistols, the Bailes over/under, and the Mongol bow and quiver of arrows. The bow was in its water-tight oiled case out of necessity, the laminating was subject to moisture and could easily be ruined if it were soaked.

The sudden bark of a shaft of lightning jolted Gabe, making him jerk and lean out to look. He counted again, trying to judge how far and how fast the worst of the storm was moving. He guessed it was about a quarter of an hour, maybe a little less, away. He shook his head, reached to the back of the shelter among the blankets and dragged out one of the two oilskins he had picked up in St. Louis. The trader said he had gotten them from a down-on-his-luck keelboater from New Orleans, said they were the first he'd seen. The long-tailed coats had been too cumbersome for riding and Gabe had split the tails so he could sit a saddle with it on, done the same for Cougar's and had only used them a couple times. Now he was glad he kept them in the bedrolls, of course they had mostly been used for ground covers to keep the moisture from seeping into the blankets, but tonight they had been laid aside, and he was glad.

He stuffed one of the saddle pistols in his belt, choosing the bigger weapon because the pans were water-proof, an unusual plus of the French craftsmanship. He struggled into the oilskin, his movements waking Cougar who asked, "Trouble?"

"Just the storm, wanna check on the horses an' such," answered Gabe. He leaned back and gave his woman a kiss, then crawled out into the rain. The rain had grown heavier and he saw the treetops swaying in the wind. He squinted from under his drooping hat brim and saw the rain taking on a more horizontal look. Another blast of lightning made him jerk around to see the bolt had struck in the heavy trees atop the low ridge to the north, sparks and smoke rose against the downpour. Thunder rolled across the sky, sounding like the rumble of a hundred heavy wagons drawn by massive draft horses pounding their giant hooves against the heavens, a rolling reverberation that shook the trees around him. He felt the impact of the next bolt that splintered and lit up the sky, the force of the blast pushing against his chest and making the very air he breathed smell like brimstone.

Ezra shouted from the overhang of the shelter, "Horses alright?" and both turned at the growling rumble that came on the heels of the lightning. Gabe's first thought was of a tornado, but that was unheard of in these mountains, tornados formed in the flatlands and the irregular contours and hills of the mountains prevented the wind from forming a funnel. But the growl increased and drew nearer. Gabe sheltered his eyes from the downpour, looking to the north across the clearing with the horses, saw only blackness until the lightning spoke again. The light showed the horse herd, milling about, frightened, looking for shelter but afraid of the trees. They began to move, trotting in a wide circle, following one another, needing some movement, anything to counter the ravages of the storm.

And then it hit! Great balls of ice, each half the size of his fist, fell in a flurry, instantly turning the ground white as they stacked together. Gabe felt the pounding against his head and shoulders, the felt hat doing little to protect from the deluge. He ran to the trees, put his back to the trunk of the big ponderosa, watching as the huge hailstones stripped branches, needles and leaves from the trees. The cottonwood, oak and maple nearer the lake were almost instantly stripped, the ice balls mercilessly stripping even the bark from the branches.

Cougar and Wolf scrambled from the lean-to, running to Gabe's side under the big tree, just as the shelter was flattened by the heavy load of hail. He heard the others shouting, and watched as they too ran to the trees, dragging blankets behind them. Another bolt of lightning showed at least five skeletal blue-white fingers stabbing at the timber half-way up the hillside above their camp, a shadowy tree toppled, flame licking at the exposed wood but was quickly snuffed out by the deluge. Deafening thunder clapped and stomped across the heavens, rumbling away like a stampede of crazed animals.

Gabe looked to the big clearing, saw the horses scattering and running everywhere. Nearby, the picketed saddle horses were huddled together, pushing closer to the trees. Another crash of lightning illuminated the grassy flat, the break in the trees and the trail beyond, horses everywhere, running wide-eyed and aimless, twisting, kicking, and tossing their heads in fear. But there was nothing they could do, the helpless feeling driving through Gabe like an icy knife that pierced his chest. Cougar had wrapped her arms around his waist, burying her head in his chest, and held tight. Gabe dropped his arms to hold her, pulling her close as he watched the hailstones piling up, branches, pine boughs, and more, littering the icy mass.

The raging wind drove the heavy ice balls at an angle, pounding through the canopy of the forest, stripping the trees almost bare. The group that sought shelter under the bigger of the trees were repeatedly beaten by the driving hail, as they huddled together, protecting one another. These warriors that had only known fear when charging into a bloody battle, now felt the heart-stopping angst of uncontrolled and growing fear, unlike anything they had known. The big tree with a trunk larger than a big man would reach around, proved to be little enough to protect Gabe and Cougar that now sat, holding one another, pushing against the massive trunk, Wolf laying across their feet. They had drawn their knees up, huddling tighter together with every jolt of thunder and crackling of lightning.

Ezra, Eagle, and Red Hawk had also pushed close together, Eagle pulling Red Hawk close to his chest, Ezra hunching beside them, head down and collar up, holding a blanket around the huddle. But the blanket did little to brunt the blows of each of the rock-hard ice balls. Ezra wishing he had grabbed the heavy buffalo robe instead, had folded the blanket double, but still it was little help. He looked beyond the trees, staring toward the lake and seeing with every flash of lightning white caps of waves that rose as much as six feet high, driving like a huge formation of white capped soldiers marching in unison to an unknown destination, but marching in step, nevertheless.

These were warriors, one and all, used to facing any peril, any opposition, and by sheer force or wise thought, had mounted together against any enemy, always prevailing, never failing. But now, unable to so much as resist, they stood, numb and frustrated, against an irresistible enemy, hunkering down to take the worst of the onslaught. Gabe thought that even the most staid of God's creation was taking a beating unlike any he had ever known. But he smiled at the thought that God was still in control, remembering a passage he read in Second Samuel, just that morning, *"When the waves of death compassed me, the floods of ungodly men made me afraid; The sorrows of hell compassed me about; the snares of death prevented me; In my distress I called upon the Lord, and cried to my God: and he did hear my voice out of his temple, and my cry did enter into his ears."* He smiled, quietly spoke a prayer of thanks and praise, asked for His protection, and pulled Cougar closer still, as they said "Amen."

He lifted his eyes and glanced around in the moonlight, realizing the moon had come from hiding, and knew the storm had abated. The hail had stopped, rain still fell, but the wind had lessened and the roar of the hail and more had quieted. Gabe saw the horses in the clearing, stopping, a few still milling about and some coming back into the clearing through the break in the trees. Gabe called out, "You alright over there!"

The irascible Ezra growled, "Reckon so, you?"

"Yup. A little wet, but alright." He looked down at Cougar as she smiled up at her man, pulled her close and whispered in her ear, "Love you!" Her arms were still about his waist and she pulled tight, lifting her face for a kiss and Gabe gladly complied.

25 / ROUND-UP

With the first light, the damage and desolation began to show. Trees stood naked, skeletal reminders of what they once were, the thicker woods of pines and fir still showed patches of green, with perky ponderosa, usually stretching high above the rest, now mostly bald at the top, long branches hanging bare, almost devoid of the usual long needles that contrasted with the rusty red bark. Oak brush, berry bushes, and tall grasses, now humbled with bare, bent, and broken branches and stalks, hanging low to the ground. The Larch, with its softer needles and smaller cones, had been stripped of most of the growth. Only the fir and some of the spruce with the short tight needles and irregular branches, still held any semblance of their former appearance, showing the only dark green of the forest. Even the strong and straight spruce, stood bare, the thin bark embarrassed and showing red with deep pock marks from the ice balls.

All the saddle horses, still picketed, hung their heads, their rumps and shoulders showing wounds and bruises from the tortuous hailstones. Worst of all was the strawberry roan of Cougar Woman, splotches of hide showed bare, some showing blood, bruises darkening as she turned to look at Cougar, eyes sad, head hanging, not understanding. Cougar Woman went to her four-legged friend and wrapped her arms around her neck, speaking softly to her, stroking her neck and head. She untied the lead rope and led her to the water at the stream, still rushing past but less than before, a pool forming as it bent around a rock. The gelding dipped his nose in the water and took a long drink, lifted his head, and turned to look at Cougar Woman. She stroked his neck again and led him, noticing a slight limp with his left rear leg, into the grassy flat, away from the wet and sat down to let the gelding snatch some grass and soak up the warmth from the rising sun.

The others had followed her lead and led their horses to water and to the grass, examining the animals as they were close, noting all had suffered from the storm and would take some time to recover. Gabe sat beside Cougar Woman and asked, "Any ideas what we can use to help those wounds?" nodding to the horses and the welts from the hail.

"I saw some plants along the stream and near the

trees that I could make a poultice with, but the wounds will need to be open to heal."

"I was afraid of that. So, I reckon we'll be walkin' for a few days."

"Unless there are some in the herd that were not hurt as bad," offered Cougar.

Gabe nodded, lifted his eyes to look at the horses that were once again grazing in the wide-open clearing, but the grass no longer stood tall, although the horses did not seem to mind. Gabe rose, motioned for Ezra to join him and they walked through the herd, looking for uninjured horses they might use for the round-up of the others, but their search was unsuccessful. "I reckon our horses, tethered in the trees as they were, didn't get hit as hard as the rest of these," suggested Ezra, nodding toward the animals that milled about in the downed grass.

"Yeah, and that means we get to do a lot o' walkin'," declared Gabe. They returned to the others and began to explain, "Looks like all the herd was hit pretty hard, scattered about as they were, but that means we are afoot." He nodded to Red Hawk, "How 'bout you staying with Cougar, help her find the plants and such to make the poultices and then you can help her take care of our horses. The rest of us will start hoofin' it and see if we can get some o' them others back here with these, and then decide if we want to start for the village, or give it another day for the horses to heal up a mite so they can be ridden."

Spotted Eagle looked at Gabe, glanced to the horses and to his own mount, "It is good. We must care for our horses, or we will be walking a long time."

"And I'm not one for walkin' any more'n I haf'to," declared Ezra. "But if'n we're gonna do it, let's get to it!" He glanced from Spotted Eagle to Gabe and turned to go to the break in the trees that led to the trail and the lake beyond.

They saw the scattered aspen among the trees, recognizing the white barked trunks and Gabe commented, "Look at that, no more'n a handful of leaves left on those aspen."

"Ain't none of the others any better. Those larch are pretty naked, and the cottonwood and chokecherries look like a tornado come through," said Ezra.

"Well, how 'bout we split up. Ezra you go north along the trail, Eagle, you take the shoreline and I'll go south. Anything we can find, just push 'em back this way and hopefully they'll want to get back together with the herd," directed Gabe, turning away.

"Sounds reasonable, but I'll be back for sumpin' to eat when that sun gets high!" declared Ezra, laying the barrel of his rifle over his shoulder and shaking his head as he laughed and started up the trail.

Eagle grinned, waved at the others as they separated, he carried his rifle, recently taken from the Blackfoot, and started toward the shoreline.

Gabe had taken the most difficult terrain for himself, leaving Ezra and Spotted Eagle to search the sparse shoreline and the low land that held the trail and sparse timber. Gabe started to the shoulder of the line of hills that pushed into the lake, following the narrow trail that cut through a low saddle to drop off the other side. The timber here showed the same degree of damage as that around their camp, but once over the saddle, he noticed the south facing slope had escaped much of the damaging storm. Trees stood tall, showing plenty of green, aspen waved their quaking leaves in the breeze, but the vegetation near the point was down and stripped. Gabe stood atop the crest, looking into the basin that fronted the lake and lay in the shadow of a tall ridge that stretched its timbered slopes back toward the high mountains. He frowned as he looked below, recognizing the terrain and dim scars along the broad peninsula that pointed to deep water.

He sat down, laying his rifle across his lap, doffed his hat and ran his fingers through his hair. He remembered the scene from just a few days back, a smoldering destroyed village of the Kutenai, bodies strewn about, black marring the land. This was the place of the first massacre at the hands of the Blackfoot, the village where most of the horses had made their home. As he searched the land below, just beyond the village and on a grassy flat above the narrow bay, several horses grazed and cavorted in the warm sunshine. He counted at least fifteen, maybe more. The missing horses from the herd, the ones that fled the storm and instinctively returned to familiar ground.

Gabe slipped his brass telescope from the case that hung at his belt, stretched it out and looked at the horses. Satisfied they were the ones from the herd, he scanned the valley for any strays and saw other sign and damage from the storm. Although most of the valley below had been missed by the storm, the point of the ridge where he sat held naked trees and skeletal remnants of what had stood the test of time, but now would probably become a silent monument to the ravages of the storm. He paused as he looked, saw the carcass of a young bear, probably knocked unconscious by the ice balls, and then beaten to death where he lay. A doe and a fawn lay side by side, both dead, obvious wounds showing from the hail. He knew the path of the storm was probably littered with other animals that had fallen before the icy death, and there were certainly many more that limped through the woods and would probably fall prey to surviving predators.

He rose to his feet and turned back toward their camp, knowing there was much to do before they could take to the trail again. As he walked, he looked around, always enraptured by the beauty of the mountains, but now seeing the evidence of the wrath of nature, yet knowing that God's design and works were beyond his understanding and that faith in the might, power, and goodness of God would give him and the others the strength needed to prevail. He smiled and began humming, then started singing one of his favorites, a song he first heard when they visited England the year after he started at the university. *"Amazing Grace, how sweet the sound . . ."* and let the music lift his steps as he sauntered back to camp.

When Spotted Eagle and Ezra returned, they were dismayed at finding none of the missing horses, but Gabe explained what he found and Ezra asked, "Just over this ridge?" pointing behind the camp.

"Ummhmmm, just over this ridge. And most of that valley was untouched by the storm!"

"Just over this ridge," grumbled Ezra, "and we were hugging these trees like the world was comin' to an end!" He shook his head as he looked at Gabe.

Spotted Eagle added, "I thought we might be close, but in the dark it was hard to tell."

As they spoke, Cougar and Red Hawk returned, arms laden with plants, and looking a bit worse for wear. They had to wade through wet grasses, downed timber, soggy bottom land, and more, just to retrieve the necessary plants and when they neared the others, they dropped their bundles and Cougar said, "Make a poultice," and turned to their gear to get some dry clothes.

26 / FEAST

The horses responded well to the treatment, savoring the attention and the day of rest. While the horses enjoyed the reviving grass that struggled to lift to the sun, the men and Cougar tended to their gear and weapons. It was late afternoon on the day of healing that Red Hawk hurried into camp, “Many riders come!” pointing to the trail below them.

“Blackfoot?” asked Spotted Eagle, grabbing for his rifle as he stood to confront his son.

“No! I think they are Kutenai!” he declared, eliciting frowns from the others.

“Kutenai?” asked Gabe, standing with his rifle held across his middle. He glanced askance to the others, getting a shrug from Ezra and little response from Spotted Eagle. “Eagle, let’s go see these Kutenai!”

They hustled to the break in the trees at the lower end of the basin, watching the trail for the riders and had no sooner made the trees than they saw the band of warriors of the Kutenai. Gabe stepped forward, hand lifted and palm open, "Greetings Crazy Owl! What brings the great chief of the Ktunaxa to our camp?"

The band came closer, Crazy Owl leading with two warriors close behind, the others further back. Cougar Woman stepped forward to translate as Owl responded, "Spirit Bear, it is good to see you and your people unharmed by the terrible storm that came." He looked past Gabe to see the others had followed the leaders to the trees, all standing with rifles ready.

"You came all this way to see if we were hurt by the storm?" asked Gabe, frowning.

"Yes, and more," he motioned if he could get down and Gabe nodded, watching as the chief and his two warriors, probably ranking leaders of the village, slide from their mounts and walk closer. "You told of the other village of the Ktunaxa and the women that went to your village for shelter."

"Yes, there were many that came, some with children as well."

"Our village also lost men and women. My council asked us to come to your village to see if our people would choose to return to the Ktunaxa, so many coming to your village could make it difficult to feed and more."

Gabe looked past the leaders at the men behind,

saw many young men and others that numbered probably twenty or more. He looked at the chief, "With so many raiders near, you have most of your warriors here. Are you not concerned that your village could be at risk?" he paused, and let a grin tug at the corner of his mouth and a mischievous but understanding glint touch his eyes, "Or is there more to this journey?"

The old chief also grinned, nodded, "Yes, we have many men that do not have a woman to warm their lodge and now the village of the Salish has many more women than men to take care of them."

Spotted Eagle grinned, chuckling a little and said, "It is good to have so many more men to take the horses to our village. Our chief, Plenty Bears, will order a big feast and dance to celebrate, a good time to make new friends!"

Smiles spread among the rest of the band as Cougar Woman spoke the translation loudly, and Gabe motioned for the others to get down. "Let's go to our camp, share a meal, and talk. We will not leave until first light and the horses need rest."

Black Badger, the young man befriended by Red Hawk, nodded to his friend and as the two started to talk, Gabe suggested, "How 'bout you two see if you can find us a deer or two, I saw several down off that point yonder, and we could use some more meat." The two grinned, and trotted off together, leading Badger's pony behind them.

The return of their own and the arrival of so many visitors caused quite a commotion in the village of the Salish. The group had been seen when they rounded the point of the bay that reached to the west. When they neared the end of the ridge, the villagers gathered at the northernmost point and lined the trail as they came into view. Spotted Eagle led with Crazy Owl at his side, Gabe and the others close behind. The men of the Kutenai pushed the herd and Spotted Eagle directed Red Hawk and the others to take the herd to the south end of the camp with the rest of the village horses.

Gabe, Cougar and Ezra broke off as the herd neared the trail that led up the shoulder of the ridge to their camp and they ducked through the trees to find their way home. Grey Dove stood before the entryway to the tipi with Stands Tall, the mother of the twins at her side, as her family rode into camp. Ezra was the first to the ground as he took two long strides to grab his woman up and spin her around as they greeted one another. As Gabe stepped down, he noticed the twins who had been seated on the blankets, were standing, and looking to the trail as if expecting someone. Cougar noticed them also and stepped near to say, "He has returned and is taking the horses to the herd. He will be returning to the lodge soon." She grinned as she saw both girls smile broadly and look to their mother.

Stands Tall had heard Cougar and nodded to her girls, who quickly grabbed their things and disappeared down the trail to the village.

Cougar was quick to pick up her youngest, and while holding him close, she dropped to her knees beside Bobcat and drew him into a tight hug. Gabe watched her, shaking his head as he was again amazed that a woman, who was such a fierce fighter and warrior, could also be such a tender loving mother and wife, but he was thankful.

The men tended the animals as the women fussed with the children. Cougar told of the Ktunaxa men and the possibility of a celebratory feast and dance. She looked at the sky, saw the lowering sun showing it to be late afternoon, and said, "I think Spotted Eagle and Plenty Bears will have that feast this night." She glanced to Stands Tall, saw the excitement of seeing and meeting more of her people, and added, "Stands Tall, perhaps you would like to help your twins prepare for the feast and dance?"

The Ktunaxa woman smiled and nodded, "Yes, I should," and rose to leave. Both Cougar and Dove thanked her and her girls for the help they had been in Cougar's absence and offered her a front quarter of the hanging venison for them to prepare for the feast. She accepted and hurried away to return to the borrowed lodge of Red Hawk. Cougar looked to Grey Dove, "What do you think the twins will do about Red Hawk?"

"You mean because now that the Ktunaxa have men here?"

"Yes. They were no doubt taken with Red Hawk, but when there is more of a choice . . ."

"Choice is good, but I think they have already decided and I think Red Hawk has also decided."

"Which one?" asked Cougar.

"Both," snickered Dove, eliciting a giggle from Cougar.

"What are you women laughin' 'bout now?" asked Gabe, dropping to the ground beside his woman on the buffalo robe where the little ones cavorted about.

"The same thing women always talk about when their men are away," declared Grey Dove, motioning Ezra close.

"And just what might that be?" asked Gabe.

"That is not for you to know!" declared Cougar, dismissively.

Ezra looked around, "Where's the coffee?"

"There," nodded Grey Dove toward the pot that sat behind a rock, the edge resting in the coals.

Ezra stood and went to the firepit, snatched up a cup, looked at Gabe with eyebrows raised in a question, received a nod, and poured two cups of steaming coffee. He handed one off to Gabe and plopped down beside Dove, stretching out to lean on one elbow and watch the little ones. Dove listened as Ezra told of the past few days, minimizing the fights, but using the time to include his woman in the happenings she had not been able to join. For this family shared everything, whether present or not, including one another in each event, for even those that stay behind are just as much a part of the adventure, though their part was not seen but appreciated, nonetheless.

Ezra was just finishing his telling of the tale when Red Hawk came through the trees, a somber expression painting his face. He looked at his friends, and plopped down beside them, shaking his head as he looked at Gabe, "What should I do?"

Gabe frowned, "Do? About what?"

"The feast and the dance," he answered, grumbling.

"You're gonna hafta explain a little about that," replied Gabe, thinking he knew what was coming, but thought it best to let Red Hawk explain.

"All the others will be there, and they are Ktunaxa!"

"Does this have to do with the twins?" asked Cougar.

Red Hawk glanced at Cougar, nodded, and grumbled, "Yes. They will not want to stay here if the men of the Ktunaxa want them."

Cougar smiled, glanced at Dove, and said, "The Salish and the Kutenai have long been friends, and it is not unusual for them to marry into the other families."

"But . . ." stuttered Red Hawk, unsure of what to say or do, obviously quite concerned about the possible loss of his newfound love.

"There are two of them. Perhaps one will choose to stay," offered Grey Dove.

"Which one?" asked Hawk, looking up at Dove.

"Both of them talked about you while you were gone, both seemed very taken with you. But I do not know which one would choose to stay. Which would you want to stay?" she asked.

"Running Fox, no, Little Rabbit, no, I don't know!" answered the exasperated young man.

Gabe grinned at Ezra and looked back at Red Hawk, "What about Stands Tall, has she said anything?"

Red Hawk looked up at Gabe, "No, but . . . I do not know," he mumbled, shaking his head, and picking up a stick to toss to the fire ring.

"Has your father's wife completed the blanket?" asked Cougar Woman.

Red Hawk looked at Cougar, frowning, and remembered about the blanket used in courting, and nodded, "I think so, but I have not been to their lodge since we returned."

"Then perhaps . . ." started Cougar, but Red Hawk jumped up and looked from one to the other, "I must go!" he declared, and scurried to the trail to return to the village. The others looked from one to another, and all started laughing together.

27 / FEAST

It was a joyous time, ample food of many varieties and people enjoying the company of new acquaintances. Sign language was the norm and fingers, and hands flew like so many locusts, flittering about, unspoken words expressed by contorted images. But the mood was light and happy, and when the drums and flutes began, the people began to dance. It was an opportunity for many to show off their best apparel, beaded and decorated dresses and tunics, porcupine roaches and headdresses, feathered fans, bells, handheld drums and more. The steady cadence of the drummers and the uplifted chants and songs filled the air and men and women shuffled and danced, making a big circle around the drums in the center.

Everything was happening in the central compound of the village, old timers sitting around the edges, just in front of the nearby hide lodges, some using willow back rests, others sitting on blankets, many chattering among friends, others using sign to speak to visitors. The early dances had more of the older couples joining together, dancing side by side, often touching or holding hands as they moved. Gabe and Cougar made a few turns of a dance, stepping away from the circle to tend to the little ones while Ezra and Dove took their turn. The women were in their finest, white buckskin dresses gaily decorated by beaded designs, rows of elk teeth, long fringe with tufts of feathers at the tips, and a row of trade bells. Each was unique and beautiful, making their men proud of the beautiful women.

As the dance continued and the hour grew late, most of the older couples sat around the circle, watching the younger people dance. While the young ones were more hesitant and uncertain in the early hours, the example set by the couples had encouraged them to join in the festivities, and once started, they reveled in the fun and excitement. Gabe elbowed Cougar, nodding to the circle of dancers where they saw Red Hawk dancing between the twins, all three obviously happy and enjoying their time together. It was the custom among the people that young people could not be alone together, and a dance was the rare opportunity to be close and talk, even touch, without the presence of a family member.

The drummers finished a song, stopped, and stood

to take a short break, giving the dancers a chance to pair off and be together, but only within the circle of light of the fires. Cougar nudged Gabe, "Look," nodding to the far side of the circle, "there are others talking with the twins and their mother, Stands Tall."

Gabe saw the small group, searched for Red Hawk, and saw him walking toward them, a somber expression showing in the firelight. He sat beside Gabe, "I do not know what to do. It is hard to talk with them using sign, and our words are few. But they," nodding to the young men talking with the twins, "have the same tongue. I think they will leave."

Gabe waited quietly a moment, "When I first met the woman I chose, I did not know her tongue and had to use sign. But before long, we were both talking in the other's language. It just takes time," he encouraged.

"There is no time. The Ktunaxa will leave after first light."

Cougar leaned close, "Then perhaps you should do something tonight."

Red Hawk frowned, "What can I do?" and pointed with his chin to the others that were talking with the girls.

"There is still time to dance, but did you not get a flute from the Shaman, Raven's Wing?"

Red Hawk leaned forward to look around Gabe to Cougar, "Yes, I got a flute and I have learned to use it."

"And you have the blanket?"

"Yes."

"Then perhaps the time to use the flute and the blanket is tonight, after the dance," suggested Cougar Woman, leaning back beside her man, smiling.

Gabe looked down at his woman, saw the expression on her face, and shook his head, knowing it was the way of women to encourage others to the union that make a family. He smiled, remembering the expression of his mother who called it, 'Playing Cupid', after the ancient Roman god of love who was said to be the son of Mercury, the winged messenger of the gods, and Venus, the goddess of love. He looked at Ezra, muttered, "They just can't help themselves. Whenever they see a young man that's not married, they do everything to get the deed done!"

"And when that happens, a man has no chance!" declared Ezra, chuckling. "Not that we'd want one, mind you!"

Gabe guessed it to be about midnight as they walked back to their camp from the festivities. He carried Bobcat, head on his shoulder as Cougar packed Fox. Ezra and Dove followed with their two little ones, also sound asleep. It had been a fun time and they met many of the Ktunaxa, some having decided to stay with the Salish, others leaving with the men from the upper village. Cougar looked at Gabe, whispered,

"Did you see where Red Hawk went?"

"No, there were too many going different directions to keep track of any of 'em."

"Do you think he will go to his lodge to see the twins?"

"Dunno, not my concern."

Cougar stopped, turned to face Gabe, and frowned, "He is a friend and you should be concerned," she scolded.

"Look, if he was in a fight and I could help, I would. But his life is not in danger, so . . ." he shrugged and started back up the trail.

Cougar shook her head, a little exasperated with her man who did not understand the way of young people, and muttered behind him as he walked, "But his life *will* be changed."

"Prob'ly," answered Gabe, yawning, and stretching after putting Bobcat down on the blankets in the tipi.

Ezra and Dove ducked into the entry, looked at the little ones and gently placed theirs nearby, also on the blankets, then covered them all, tucking the blankets around them. The women had stepped to the side and were whispering with one another, very animated in their discussion. Ezra looked at Gabe, "What's that all about?"

"Love," shrugged Gabe, going to his blankets.

"Oh, that," mumbled Ezra, also going to his blankets on the far side of the lodge.

Red Hawk looked across the lodge to his father's wife, Prairie Flower, listening as she spoke. "You must be respectful of their mother. If she speaks, you obey." She looked from under her brows to the young man, giving the age-old mother stare to a young man, "It will be the choice of the young woman. If she chooses to come out, then you may step forward, but not until then." She gave him the glare again as he nodded his understanding. She stood and stretched out her hands with the blanket, newly finished and decorated for the purpose. Red Hawk smiled as he accepted the folded blanket, holding it one-handed, stroking the patchwork cloth as he admired the handiwork. Of several colors and sewn together blankets, it was decorated with long strips of fur and beadwork, showing special care and craftsmanship. Prairie Flower had solicited the help of four of her friends, women who were excited to make a courting blanket for the son of the war leader of the Salish people.

Red Hawk looked up at Prairie Flower, "I am grateful. This is beautiful."

"Honor the tradition of our people as you go with it," she stated as she turned away to dismiss the young man.

He stepped from the lodge, looked to the sky and the waning moon, but seeing all the brightness of the clear night with the stars winking and blinking as if illuminating the way to the lodge where Stands Tall and her twin daughters would be, although they did not know he was coming with a special purpose on his mind. It was a cool night, yet he felt a trickle of sweat course its way down his back, making him shiver in the night air. He touched the flute in his belt, trying to remember what he must do, each step taking him nearer and his heart beating faster. He thought of what he must do, certain of his purpose, but uncertain of which girl would respond, if either. He had a flitting thought that they might have already committed to one of the men from the Kutenai village, then cast it aside, believing the woman of his choice would be waiting.

A scrawny dog scampered away from him, ducking behind a lodge, tail between his legs. A great horned owl asked his lonesome question of the darkness, and behind him at water's edge, the cry of a loon was answered by another further out on the water. The dim light of the half-moon cast a hint of pale blue upon the grey hide lodges, some with a tendril of smoke curling from the high-up flaps. The smell of smoke, dust, pines, and the slight fishy smell of the big lake, wafted before him, the familiarity giving him comfort as he struggled with his plan. He had no idea what he would say if one of the girls came from the lodge, but he knew what he would feel if they ignored his overture.

He shook his head, thinking he should forget this and just wait till they left, then move back into the lodge, after all, it was his lodge. But he continued, breathing deeply with every step, rehearsing what he was to do, fearful it would make him feel the fool. But he continued. As he neared the lodge, the flap had been thrown back, the light from the interior fire gave a glow to the hide lodge and a brightness to the entry. But no one was about and Red Hawk thought they must be inside, then had another thought that made him look about, fearful of seeing the girls walking with another man, but there was no one. He sucked in a deep breath that lifted his shoulders, making him grab for the blanket that hung there, then settled down and reached for the flute.

28 / COURTING

Red Hawk stood away from entry of the lodge, well out of the light from within, but alone in the area before the lodge. The blanket hung from his shoulders, and he brought the flute to his lips. He rehearsed in his mind what he was to play, then looked to the lodge and began. The lonesome wail of the flute lifted above the tipi and the village, wafting about on the night breeze, clear notes that sounded almost eerie in the darkness, but hauntingly appealing. The sound lifted and fell, twittering and warbling, painting images of beautifully colored birds singing a courtship song and it paused as Red Hawk breathed deep and continued.

He caught his breath as he saw a shadow at the entry, then continued the melody of love, hoping for more. A figure, shadowed by the fire from within, ducked through the entry and stood to one side. Red Hawk finished the song, letting the last note trail off into the night, then slipped the flute behind his belt, looked at his feet then lifted his eyes to see who stood before the lodge. The entry cover was pushed aside and more light came from within, only to be shadowed again as another figure came from the light to stand beside the entry.

Red Hawk stepped forward, still unable to see who stood before him, but he slowly opened his arms, holding the blanket wide to either side and stopped, waiting, feeling his heart pounding as if the dance continued and the drums came from within. He looked at the two beside the entry, fearing one was Stands Tall, the mother, for whatever reason she might think proper. Then both figures, side by side, slowly came forward. As they neared, the moonlight revealed the broad smiles of both girls, hand in hand, coming to Red Hawk. As they neared, they separated, one on either side of the young man, and stepped into the blanket. Red Hawk breathed, realizing he had been holding his breath, and closed the blanket around them, drawing them closer.

His mind was racing, his heart rapidly beating, and he wondered, *Is this real? Are they both here? Is this possible?* He dismissed the questions, drew the young women close as they turned to face him, side by side. They looked up at him and he turned from one to the other, "Is this what you want? Both of you? To be mine always?"

They smiled, nodding their heads and Running Fox said, "We have talked of this, it is what we both hoped would be." Little Rabbit nodded as Running Fox spoke and added, "We have talked with our mother about this and she said it is good for us to be joined to the same man together and she knows you are a good man."

In the custom of their people, there was no special ceremony required for a wedding to be complete. The act of coming to the man and being accepted into his blanket was considered the joining of separate lives becoming one. The taking of more than one wife was seldom done at the same time, it was usually a step taken when a sister or friend would be added as a second wife as much for the benefit of the woman getting a helper as for the man gaining another wife. However, it was usually only allowed when the man was proven as a warrior and provider able to protect and provide for another member of the family.

Red Hawk had never thought of both girls becoming his wives, his concern was how to choose one or the other, but now his thoughts turned to another and he asked girls, "What about your mother? Will she stay with us?"

Running Fox giggled, "One of the men that came from the upper village was the brother of our father. He has asked our mother to come to his lodge as his woman. His wife was killed by the Blackfoot."

The three were walking together, enjoying the night

air and the time to talk and learn more about one another. The women had their arms around Red Hawk's waist and his were around theirs, the blanket held tight around the three. Little Rabbit looked at Red Hawk, "We heard some talk about the last few days and the fight with the Blackfoot. Would you tell us more?"

Red Hawk nodded, asked what they heard, and added enough to tell of the fight and the storm, without focusing on his part. It was not an accepted way of the people for one to brag of his own exploits, but to allow others to tell of the great deeds and more. He knew more would be told, but he wanted to know more about the girls, everything he could learn was important to him.

They came to a bit of a clearing beside the trail that overlooked the flats where the horses grazed and they stopped, found a place to be seated together beside the trail and talked. When one of the girls said, "I am thankful the Great Spirit has brought us together."

Red Hawk smiled and said, "There is something I must tell you. Something I learned from our good friends, Spirit Bear and Cougar Woman, and the others." He began to tell them of the hard winter that the Blackfoot attacked their village and captured several young people. He explained about his father's wounds, how he was sent to tell Spirit Bear, and how he helped to rescue the captives.

He continued, "Because it was a hard winter and

some were unable to travel, Spirit Bear and Cougar Woman kept us through the winter in their cabin. While we were there, we learned many things; the language of the Blackfoot, the Nez Percé, the English of the white man, how to read the tracks in the white man's book, and more." He paused, looking from Fox to Rabbit, and their upturned faces and wide eyes said they wanted to know more, and he continued.

"You spoke of the Great Spirit, and the white man believes in the Great Spirit or Creator as we do, but there is more. When one of our people is killed, we speak of him crossing over to the other side, some people tell of the great way," pointing to the Milky Way that pillared in the night sky, "but the tracks in the white man's book called the Bible tell of what they call Heaven."

"Heaven?" asked Running Fox, frowning.

"Yes, but it also tells us how we can know that we will go to Heaven," said Red Hawk, looking from one to the other. "I can tell you if you want to know."

Little Rabbit asked, "This Heaven, is it the same as what we have thought of as the Other Side?"

"Yes, but it is even more and all of us that stayed with Spirit Bear and Cougar Woman learned of these things and did as the Bible says."

The girls frowned, but leaned closer, wanting to know more and Running Fox asked, "Did everyone do as this Bible says to know about Heaven?"

Red Hawk smiled, "It tells all about Heaven, but it is not just to know about it, but to know that when we cross over, we will go to Heaven and live forever with the Creator God."

"Can we know this?" asked Little Rabbit.

"Yes, I will tell you." Red Hawk leaned back and began to explain, using both sign and what few words of their languages that were similar, what he knew and what he had told others as he learned from the Bible. He started by telling about the wonders of Heaven as described in the Bible, the presence of God, the choirs of angels, and more. Then he spoke of the eternal place with streets of gold, gates of pearl, and the river of life. The girls listened, eyes wide with wonder, and the Red Hawk began to tell what they must know and believe to go to Heaven.

"As I learned, what we must know is that we are all sinners, *Rom. 3:23,* you know, that we have done wrong things." The girls nodded, looking to one another and understanding, then looked back to Red Hawk as he continued, "And because of those bad things, the punishment is to die and go to Hell forever, *Rom. 5:12, 6:23.* But God does not want us to do that, so he made a way to escape, and that is to send his Son, Jesus, to pay that punishment for us."
"You mean the great Creator had a son, and made him pay for what I did that was bad?" asked Running Fox.

"Yes, He did."

"Why?" asked Little Rabbit.

"Because He loves us so much, so His son, Jesus, died for us, and when He did, he paid for the greatest gift, the gift to live forever, just for us! *Rom. 5:8, 6:23.* But," he paused to look at each of the girls, "It is like any gift, you must believe and accept that gift." He looked from one to the other, saw a look of confusion in their eyes, and explained, "If I have a gift for you," he paused and withdrew his knife from the sheath, held it out before him, holding it by the blade, the haft and handle toward them, "if this is a gift, you can look at it, believe it is a real knife, believe the knife is sharp and useful, but," he paused again, waiting, "until you take it from my hand, accept it, it will not be yours and you cannot use it, no matter how much you believe in it."

He took a deep breath, then added, "The gift of eternal life is like that. We must believe with our heart," he touched his chest with his closed fist, "that it is real. And then we must ask for that gift and accept it from God."

"How do we do that?" asked Little Rabbit.

"Just like you would ask me for the knife. You just ask, believing you will receive it, and accept it. When we speak to the Great Spirit, Creator, God, we do that in prayer. So, if you want to, I will pray aloud, you can repeat what I say, but only if you mean it and believe it with your heart, and accept that gift so you will know that when you cross over, you will go to

Heaven. Do you want to do that?"

The girls looked at one another, nodded, and looked back at Red Hawk, smiling, and reaching for his hands. "Yes," they said together.

Red Hawk bowed his head and began praying, "Our Father in Heaven, your Bible tells us to pray and ask you for that greatest gift, eternal life." He continued, expressing the desire of the girls to know Heaven, then led them to pray, "Now if you believe with all you have, and want to pray, then just repeat this prayer after me, . . . *Dear Father, I know I am a sinner and have done wrong. I believe you sent Jesus to pay for my sin and give us the gift to live in Heaven forever. Please forgive me of my sin, and give me that gift of eternal life, so I can live in Heaven with you forever. In Jesus name I pray. Amen."* As he prayed, then paused, the girls repeated each phrase after him, until he said Amen. They looked up smiling, and the three hugged one another, happy to know they would one day be in Heaven together forever.

Red Hawk looked at the moon, reckoned it to be well after midnight, and stood, the girls standing with him, and started for the lodge. In the way of the people, they were now joined together as in marriage, and Red Hawk would stay in the lodge tonight and hereafter. They talked and laughed as they made their way back to what would be their home, happy together, knowing they would be a family.

29 / RIVAL

Red Hawk, when he spent the winter in the cabin, had followed the example of Gabe and Ezra and established the habit of meeting with his Lord early in the morning, usually before first light and in an isolated place. He rolled from his blankets early, stood above the sleeping women and smiled. He ducked through the entry and using the light of the stars and lowering moon, made his way to a shoulder of the ridge overlooking the camp for his time of prayer and thanksgiving, knowing he had much to be thankful for on this day.

From his promontory, almost three hundred feet above the valley floor, he had an overarching view of the village and the low ridge on the east side. The tall ridge behind him rose like a protective monolith, offering shelter and cover for the encampment. As he finished his quiet time, he stood, facing the pale grey in the eastern sky that shadowed the lower eastern ridge and foretold the coming sunrise. He walked down the faint game trail, turned toward the lake when he dropped to the main trail that led from the lake to the south end of the valley where the horse herd grazed. He turned into the scattered juniper and oak brush that held the path around the encampment and looked to the lodges, saw some activity as women worked to start their cookfires and begin the chores of the day.

As he passed several lodges, he saw some horses before his lodge, frowning, he quickened his step. Three men, six horses, stood before his lodge, the older man speaking loudly and gesticulating as he stood, menacing in his manner, talking to Stands Tall, the mother of the twins. Behind her stood the twins, obviously frightened and glaring at the other men. As he neared, the twins saw him first and spoke to their mother, who stopped talking and looked at Red Hawk. She turned to speak to the older man, pointing toward Red Hawk as he came near.

Red Hawk looked at Running Fox and Little Rabbit, lifted his shoulders, hands at his side open and held out, asking what was happening. Fox rapidly used sign to try to explain, Little Rabbit speaking as she did, hoping for Hawk's understanding. A quick glance to the side told Hawk others were watching, and he stepped forward to stand between the women and the men. The older man glared at Red Hawk, used sign as he spoke, "We come for the women! They will go with us to the village of the Ktunaxa!"

Red Hawk scowled, asked, "Who are you?"

"I am Little Bear, the brother of the man that was her mate," pointing with his chin to Stands Tall. "She has agreed to come to our village and will be my mate!"

"She told us of this. But why do you have three other horses? And why are you arguing with her," nodding toward Stands Tall.

"Her daughters will come with her! They are Ktunaxa and will come to be with their people! They are her family; I am the head of this family and what I say will be done!" The two younger men with him nodded and grumbled their agreement, both looking toward the twins and glowering.

Red Hawk frowned as he recognized his friend, Black Badger, but turned back to the older man. "You are nothing but the brother of the man that was her mate. You could not protect her and her people, they came to the Salish for protection! Until you are properly joined with this woman, you have nothing to say!"

The man stepped forward, his stance showing his threat, and growled, "You are Salish!" he spat the words with contempt, "You have nothing to say! Move away before I show you what a real warrior will do with a boy!"

Red Hawk lifted his head proudly, "You? A real warrior? You ran and hid when your village was attacked by a handful of Blackfoot! Because you ran away, many of your people died! This warrior," beating on his chest with his fist, "and my friends, this many!" he held up his hand, all fingers extended, within inches of the man's face, "went against all the warriors that destroyed your village while you were hiding, and killed them all!" He spat at the man's feet and stepped back; arms crossed over his chest.

The young warrior beside Black Badger, shouted and stepped beside the older man, glared at Red Hawk, "If you do not want to die, move away. The women are coming with us!"

The men had been so focused on one another, they missed the movement of the twins. Two arrows thudded into the ground at the feet of the men, causing them to step back and look up as the twins each nocked a second arrow, and looked at the men. They stood silently, letting their arrows say what needed to be said. The older man looked at the twins, then turned toward Stands Tall, shook his head, and started to turn but was stopped by the voice of Spotted Eagle from behind them.

Chief Plenty Bears stood beside Spotted Eagle and Gabe and Cougar Woman stepped from the side of the lodge, as Spotted Eagle said, and Cougar translated,

"We fought against our enemy the Blackfoot because they had attacked your villages. Our people have been allies, we have saved your women that were captives, and those that came for refuge, and this is how you repay our people?"

Little Bear looked at the chief and war leader, turned to face them and started, "This woman was the wife of my brother. It is the way of our people for the brother to take the woman into his lodge and provide for her and the family of my brother. I spoke to her of this, she agreed, but now that I come for her, they will not come! She says this boy has claimed the girls as his wives, but this cannot be, I will not allow it!"

"This man is a proven warrior of the Salish people and fought against the Blackfoot that destroyed your village while you were hiding in the trees! As a warrior of the people, he has done as our custom demands and properly taken these women as his wives. They were not taken captive, they were not forced, but made that decision as they wanted. They were under the protection of the Salish and lived in the lodge of this man who provided for them. They are bound only by the custom of our people!" stated Spotted Eagle. He paused as he looked past the man, asked the women, "Did you choose to take this man as your mate?"

Both nodded yes but did not change their stance with the bows held at their waist, arrows nocked.

Eagle looked at Stands Tall, "Do you want this man for your mate?" nodding toward Little Bear.

Stands Tall looked from Eagle to Little Bear, who turned toward her, anger flaring in his eyes, his lip curling in a threatening snarl. She looked back to Spotted Eagle, "If Red Hawk will allow, I will stay in this lodge," and dropped her eyes.

Eagle stepped back before Little Bear and said, "It is the custom of our people if you want to challenge this warrior for these women, it will be done."

Red Hawk stepped forward to show his willingness to fight, glaring at the man and with a quick glance to the others. Little Bear looked at Red Hawk, then to the women, mumbled and went to his horse. He swung aboard his mount, looked at Stands Tall, "You have made your choice! My duty is done!" He jerked the head of his horse around, a glower at the two with him was all the order they needed to follow him, but Plenty Bears stopped them with an uplifted hand. With a nod to the extra horses, obviously brought for the women, he ordered, "Leave the horses!"

They dropped the leads and dug heels to the ribs of their mounts to kick them into a gallop and stormed through the village, shouting their war cries as they left. To ride a horse through the village at a run is considered an insult and several warriors that had gathered nearby looked to their chief for permission to go after the fleeing Kutenai, but he stopped them. "Let them go! They have been chased away by women of their own people, they will never forget that, nor will their own people. They will be shamed!"

The chief and Spotted Eagle looked at Red Hawk and the women, nodded with a bit of a grin, and turned away to go to their own lodges. Gabe and Cougar Woman started to leave, but Stands Tall spoke, "If it is acceptable with the man of this lodge," nodding toward Red Hawk, "It would be good for you to join us for our meal."

Cougar looked at Gabe, then back to Stands Tall and nodded, "It is good," she said, and offered to help, motioning Gabe to be seated with Red Hawk. The men sat on the blanket that lay before the fire circle and Gabe said, "So, two wives, huh?" grinning.

Red Hawk dropped his eyes, "I did not expect that, but they both came from the lodge when I played the flute. They said their mother thought it was good." He paused, looked up at Gabe, "I read in the Bible where many men had more than one wife. Is it not a good thing?"

Gabe grinned, knowing this was a discussion that would accomplish little but to add more confusion and simply agreed, "Yes, there were many in the old days that had more than one wife, but they couldn't shoot arrows like those two." He looked up at Red Hawk, "Now it's probably easy, but wait until you can understand their language. It might get a little more, shall we say, challenging?"

They watched at the four women fussed over two men but enjoyed the attention and the meal was good. The women were already understanding one another and they often laughed together, Gabe catching Cougar's mischievous smile and knew she was enjoying the time together with the new wives of Red Hawk.

30 / RETURN

"I am concerned for my son and his women," began Spotted Eagle as he and Gabe walked along the trail toward the horse herd, Wolf between them. They were going to check on their horses, and those of the Kutenai herd, but it was a time when Eagle could speak freely with his friend.

"Because of the Ktunaxa?"

"Yes. Little Bear has been shamed and the two with him as well. The only way he can regain respect, is to take the women from Red Hawk."

"Do you think they will try to come into the camp to take the women?" asked Gabe, incredulously, thinking of three men against the entire camp of Salish.

"When a warrior loses the respect of his people, there is nothing more important that have it restored. Some turn renegade and leave their village to make their own way, but that is hard, unless they find others to join. Even his lodge belonged to his woman and when Stands Tall refused to go with him, he lost all claim to the lodge and the things within. Others that claimed his woman as their family would take all he had, unless he had one of her family with him. He has lost everything."

"And the young warriors with him?"

"I do not know about them. If they have their own lodges or if they are with their family, if they were to take one of the women of Red Hawk, that would be a claim for the property of Little Bear."

"Even though they now have a mate?"

"It is no different than if they were captives of a raid on an enemy camp. The women could be made wives or slaves depending on the warrior who takes them."

"And you think they'll try something soon?"

Eagle stopped and looked into the valley at the milling herd of horses, thought for a moment and looked at Gabe, "Yes. It has only been one day, and Little Bear might believe if he takes them before returning to the village, his people will not learn of his shame."

They started walking again, going to the upper end of the valley. The horse herd was scattered but would stay within the area where grass was high and fresh water plentiful, though some curious animals might wander into the thicker trees and become prey for bears, cougars, and wolves. They walked in silence for a while until Eagle spotted a large flat boulder that sat in the sun and offered an invitation for rest. It was a clear day, the cloudless sky shone brilliant blue and the sun was warm, dropping into the west and stretching for the jagged horizon. With the warmth on their backs, the men sat watching the herd before them, looking for their own animals. Although both men kept their favorite horse near their lodge, the other animals mingled with the herd and they picked them out, watching each one for any sign of injury or need.

"If they were to return and find the women gone and warriors waiting . . ." started Eagle, verbalizing his thoughts, though not a complete plan.

"Perhaps we should speak with Red Hawk," suggested Gabe, glancing at Spotted Eagle.

Eagle nodded, rose from the boulder and the men started back to the village.

"But what about the women?" asked Red Hawk, "Where will they be?"

"They could go to our lodge," suggested Gabe, "it is apart from the rest of the village and not easily seen, and," chuckling as the thought filled his mind, "that bunch of women could fight off a band of grizzlies!" The others laughed at the thought of any grizzly being dumb enough to go against the likes of Cougar Woman and four angry women.

Red Hawk looked at his father, "Do you think they

will be back so soon?"

"It is the best way for Little Bear to keep his respect," replied Eagle. "If he were to return to their village without Stands Tall and her daughters, he would be shamed. Since he did not come back for them last night, this would be the time for his return."

"Little Bear is mine!" declared Red Hawk, spitting the name of the man who would destroy his family.

Eagle nodded, glanced at Gabe and back. "It is good."

The waning moon was a little less than half, but the clear night provided a stage for the moon and stars to dance in concert, the stars showing the brilliance of the summer lanterns. The milky way stood like a pillar of heaven, arrayed in the multi-hued colors of its robe of darkness. The lodge of Red Hawk stood near the south edge of the camp, other lodges nearby but none closer than six or seven yards. Inside were the blanketed forms of Red Hawk, Spotted Eagle, and Gabe with the dark fur coat of Wolf lying against the edge of the inner lining of the tipi. Outside, Ezra stood his watch above the camp, looking for any movement that showed in the dim light of the moon.

Ezra glanced to the moon, guessed the time to be just after midnight, the time he would choose if he were to try to enter a village for dastardly purposes. He sat on the rocky promontory that offered a good view of the entire camp, high enough to see over the hide lodges and into the midst of the village. He let his eyes roam the perimeter of the camp, knowing he would more likely see something with the periphery of his vision than within his direct sight. He searched the far edge at the base of the long low ridge, then the lower end of the camp near the lakeshore. As he turned slightly to take in the near side toward the point of the tall ridge, he caught movement. He paused, watching, and three riders came from the point, following the trail that flanked the ridge and would lead to the upper end of the encampment or on to the horse herd.

When he was certain these were the expected Ktunaxa, he lifted the cry of the nighthawk, the raspy peent repeated twice. He sat still, watching from the shadows of the night. When the three left the trail, entering the village and moving between the tipis, Ezra left his promontory, his war club hung at his back, and stealthily followed.

Inside the lodge, Wolf and Gabe both lifted their heads at the familiar cry of the nighthawk, knowing Ezra's cry varied little from the actual, but still recognizable as his own. Gabe glanced to Eagle and Red Hawk, whispered, "They're coming!" and lay back down, his arm on Wolf's neck to make him lie still at his side. Within moments, the entry blanket was moved aside and laid upon the outside of the lodge, a shadowy figure stepping inside. Gabe could see through squinted eyes, but lay unmoving, until the man, obviously Little Bear, dropped to one knee beside the prone figure of Red Hawk and lifted a knife shoulder high, ready to plunge it into the body of Red Hawk.

But the young warrior was waiting, and as the blade lifted, he instantly reached for a handful of hair, and brought Little Bear's face down to meet his rising knee, smashing the intruder's nose across his face, and flattening his lips across bloodied teeth. Hawk grabbed the wrist of the hand that held the knife, pushed it back and lunged forward, driving the man to his back as he forcefully brought his knee to Little Bear's crotch in an excruciating blow, eliciting a scream from the bloody face of the attacker.

Red Hawk held his own knife at the throat of Little Bear as he pinned the man on his back, snarled through clenched teeth, "I will not kill you; you are family!" Little Bear struggled for air, blood filling his mouth and throat, he started to spit and Red Hawk pushed his face aside, keeping the knife tight against the man's throat. As Little Bear's face turned, he stared into the gaping mouth and flaming eyes of Wolf, who stood, head down, feet spread, in an attack stance, ready to rip Little Bear's throat apart. Little Bear froze, blood dripping from his mouth, gurgling as he fought for air, fear filling his eyes.

Spotted Eagle and Gabe had slipped past the struggle and stepped from the lodge, confronting the two young warriors as they stepped before them, grabbing the head stalls of the horses. Black Badger held a bow with a nocked arrow, started to lift it as Gabe stepped to the side, keeping the head of Badger's horse between them.

The other warrior held a lance and started to lean forward to thrust it into Spotted Eagle, but Eagle grabbed the shaft of the lance and pulled, unseating the young man, dropping him to the ground. Eagle flipped the lance around and before the young warrior could rise, Eagle stood with the lance point at the warrior's throat. The young man froze, lay back with arms wide, eyes flaring.

Black Badger twisted side to side, trying for a shot at Gabe, started to draw the bow for a shot, but a voice behind him came from the darkness, "I wouldn't do that!" Ezra's raspy voice uttered words that Badger did not know but understood the intent. He turned his head, saw the war club held high, looked down at Black Buffalo, and lowered the bow, replacing the arrow in his quiver.

They looked back to see a dark form emerge from the hide lodge, stumbling as he stepped from the entry, Red Hawk holding the man's hair in one hand, a knife in the other, steadied the stumbling man by jerking on his braids and stepped through the entry, Wolf at his heels. Red Hawk snarled, "This time you live. If you ever enter the village of my people again, all of you will be counted as an enemy and you will die a slow death!" He shoved Little Bear, making him stumble again, but he caught himself as he fell against his mount. "Now leave," demanded Red Hawk, "slowly and quietly, or I will let Wolf," nodding at the black snarling beast beside him, "tear you apart and eat you for his meal and chew your bones for days!"

Little Bear struggled to mount his horse, sat awkwardly atop, favoring his hurting crotch, and jerked the head of the horse around as he mumbled incoherent threats, and led the group of raiders quietly from the village. The men watched the raiders leave, then Gabe went to Wolf, "Sorry boy, I thought you were gonna get a treat, but I reckon not." He looked up at Red Hawk, "Chew your bones for days? That's rather gruesome, don'tcha think?"

The men laughed, as much in relief as at the humor of the comment, then Ezra said, "If we start now, we could prob'ly get back to our camp in time for coffee and a good meal fixed by five loving women, what say?" The men chuckled and followed Ezra as he started to the shoulder of the ridge that was catching the first hint of grey from the morning light, each one thinking about something to eat to start the day right.

31 / SUMMER

The rest of the summer was peaceful, the Blackfoot had lost too many warriors to make war on any of their traditional enemies, although there were probably some of the bands to the east that were not like the rest of the Piikani and chose to keep to themselves. The Siksika bands to the south of the Blackfoot territory were probably struggling with the drought of the southern mountains, much like Gabe and company and the Salish had experienced.

Friendly nations, like the *Ql'ispé* or Kalispel, and the Pend d'Oreille, had visited with the Salish, renewing old acquaintances. When a hunting party of the *Ql'ispé* stopped, Gabe was pleased to see their friend, Lame Bull. The Kalispel warrior recognized Gabe and pushed his mount forward to greet his friend, "Spirit Bear, Black Buffalo, it is good to see my friends."

"And you as well," answered Gabe, motioning for

the man to step down.

As he slipped to the ground, Lame Bull looked about, "This is a camp of the Salish, are you part of this band?"

Gabe grinned, "We are friends with the Salish, but our camp is back there," nodding to the tall ridge, "in the trees."

"We passed a village of the Kutenai; they spoke of a white man and a dark friend that fought the Blackfoot. I thought of you and when they told of you killing so many, I knew it was my friends."

"You must join us for a meal, Lame Bull, so we can talk of many things," offered Gabe, glancing to Ezra.

"We have far to go and must return to our village. We have been away many days and our village waits to go to our winter camp." He paused, looking at the trees and the cloudy sky, "The signs tell of an early and hard winter and we must prepare."

As they spoke, the honking of south bound geese caught their attention, prompting them to look up and to one another, nodding and grinning. Lame Bull added, "We have seen the raccoons with big tails and heavy fur, and more."

"And the elk have lost their velvet and are bugling," added Gabe, although those were not signs of a hard winter, by their starting so early told of a soon-coming winter. Elk would herd up, the bulls gather their harems and breeding would begin, bringing calves in early summer.

"Will you stay here for the winter?" asked Lame Bull, looking to Gabe.

"No, we only came north with the Salish because where our home is, there was a dry spring and drought that pushed us north. We will return soon so we too can prepare for winter."

They visited a while longer, a few of the visitors made trades, but the friends had to bid one another farewell as the hunting party started back north. As they left, Ezra looked at Gabe, "So you been thinkin' 'bout it too, huh?"

Gabe frowned, looked at his friend, "Thinkin' 'bout what?"

"Headin' back home 'fore cold weather hits."

Gabe grunted, "Yeah, I have. I'm thinkin' its gonna be a hard winter and the signs say it's comin' soon, so . . ." he shrugged. They walked back to the camp, where Dove and Cougar were putting food on for their mid-day meal and sat down near the cook fire. The women looked at their men, then one another, and Cougar asked, "When?"

Gabe frowned, "How do you do that?"

Ezra looked at Gabe, "Do what?" "You know, it's like she already knows what I'm thinkin'. I didn't say anything, and she already knows we're thinkin' 'bout goin' south."

The women looked at one another, giggled, and

Dove said, "Do we not always return home at this time?"

"Well, yeah," answered Gabe, looking askance to Cougar. His woman smiled and said, "You become restless, always looking about, wanting to do something, but do nothing. It is a sign just like the wooly worm."

Gabe frowned, "Wooly worm?"

"Yes," she answered, looking around. She went to the aspen near the upper edge of the camp, kicked some leaves about and bent to pick up a caterpillar. She brought the creature to Gabe, pointed at the colors, "When the wooly worm has a wide band of orange in the middle, it will be a mild winter. A narrow band, like this one, with black at both ends, tells of a winter with heavy snow." She looked up at Gabe as he frowned at the fuzzy thing in Cougar's palm.

Gabe looked up at Cougar, grinned and lifted his eyebrows, wrinkling his brow, "You don't say!"

Cougar frowned, "Yes, I just said it did."

Gabe chuckled, smiled, knowing his expression had confused his woman and pulled her close, hugging her and laughing. "So, I guess we need to start thinkin' about goin' south while the caterpillar still has a little orange around his middle."

Although the aspen had already started showing touches of color, within a few days it appeared as if the Creator had dipped his brush in the well of gold and began splashing the mountainsides with fall's favorite color. With touches of orange and red, the golden quakies shivered in the cooler air of fall and beckoned the group south.

Gabe and company had said their goodbyes to the Salish, who would soon follow them south, and started on the trail that brought them to the north country but would return them home. Cougar sat her strawberry roan, nestled into her saddle, with Fox in the cradleboard that hung from the pommel beside her right leg. Gabe had Bobcat in his familiar place before him, holding onto the saddle horn. Ezra had Chipmunk seated before him, and Dove had Squirrel still in a cradleboard. Although Cougar had a board for Bobcat, Gabe wanted the boy with him and would put him in the cradleboard if it became uncomfortable for either.

On the way north, they had waited a week before starting out after the Salish village, but now they would lead the way and the villagers would follow in a week or two. Gabe was usually the type of traveler that once on the trail, he totally focused on the way before him and was always searching for the familiar landmarks that would tell of home, often to the consternation of the more leisurely travelers with him. He looked back at the string of horses that trailed behind them, tethered together, and lined out. They decided to travel with the same get-up as when they came north. Ezra trailed the buckskin gelding that was harnessed with the travois carrying Dove's tipi. The mule and big grey were packed, but allowed to follow free rein, while Gabe led the Appaloosa mare and the steeldust mustang on a long lead and the Appy's colt trotted freely beside his mother, long legs flashing in the sunlight. The men would handle the horses while the women had the tougher task of tending to the children.

They had an early start, and all the animals were anxious to stretch their legs, making a quick pace and covering several miles before they settled down to a steady ground-eating walk. Everyone was enjoying the colors that were beginning to show their glory, mountainsides painted with the gold aspen, red of oak brush, orange and yellows of berry bushes and cottonwood. Pine trees were dropping cones, and cool breezes coming from the high country to chase geese and ducks to their southern waters.

Whenever the trail allowed, they traveled beside one another, but more often the game trails narrowed, and they moved into a single file column. They were stretched out in a long line, twisting through thick timber, when Gabe reined up, holding his hand high to signal the others to stop. He slipped the Ferguson rifle from the scabbard beneath his leg, and stepped down, glancing back to Ezra who did the same. When Ezra came alongside, Gabe pointed to the valley below the trail to point out a big mama grizzly facing off with a big boar. Two yearling cubs were well behind their mother, one standing and pawing the air as his mother went to her hind legs to threaten the boar. Snapping her jaws and roaring, she slapped at the air and cocked her head to the side.

The big boar lifted his head, bellowing with a growl and a roar, threatening the female as he slapped at the grass before him, feinting a charge, stepping back and opening his mouth wide to let loose a roar that bounced off the mountainside. It was not unusual for a boar to be threatened by a sow passing through, and he would often try to kill the cubs to bring the female back into season so he could breed with her. But there are few creatures, if any, that are more fearsome and mean than a mama grizzly protecting her cubs. The boar tried to feint a charge, but a vicious slap from the sow, knocked his head to the side and made him stumble. The sow charged, biting at the boar's neck, and clawing at his side.

The huge boar, hackles raised at his neck and shoulders, started to rise, but the challenge was met as the sow rose on her hind legs, slapping at the boar and growling, snapping her jaws. The boar, also standing, stepped back, growled a threat, then dropped to all fours and turned away. He started to leave, and the sow made one last charge, biting the boar's rump, making him tuck his tail and scamper away. She stood again, roared her last threat, then dropped and looked for her cubs, who scooted to her side as she sniffed at each one, and with a glance over her shoulder, she led them away and into the thick timber across the valley.

Gabe shook his head, looked up to see Ezra standing between the horses with the women mounted and watching the display in the valley bottom. The horses had been a little skittish, but with the women aboard and talking to them as they stroked their necks, they did not spook but watched the bout between the bears with the same curiosity of the women. Gabe shook his head, took the lead of Ebony from Ezra, and said, "Guess we can move on now, if it's alright with you bear gawkers." He grinned as he saw Cougar and Dove look at one another as if they didn't understand the remark, but a smile from both told Gabe they fully understood but didn't care.

Back on the trail, they headed south through the mountains, staying on the route that paralleled the hills on the west side of the long valley, but kept to the flats. As the sun lowered to the western mountains, they took to the trail that rose above the wide bend of the Salish river and took them into the narrow valley bounded by ridges to the east and west. It bent slightly to the east as it followed the river that flanked the western ridge. When the river made its dog-leg bend around the point of land to turn to the south, a grassy flat in the shade of a cluster of cottonwood beckoned, and the group yielded to the welcome sight for their camp for the night.

32 / SOUTH

The second day out of the encampment with the Salish found the family taking the southbound bend to the trail aimed to the cut that would drop them into the valley of the river of three forks. They camped in the shadow of the timbered knob that marked the line of hills that marched northwest toward the Bitterroots. Behind them rose the taller mountains of the Rockies, a long range that was known as the Salish Range, marking the eastern extent of Salish territory and the beginning of the land of the Blackfoot.

The third day they rode through the narrow cut that opened into the long valley of the three forks, the Bitterroot, the Blackfoot, and the Middle Fork. After the confluence of the rivers, the waters bore the name of the Bitterroot until it joined with the Salish. The wide valley was lush and green, no sign of the previously encroaching drought. At the forks, they crossed the gravelly bottom and wide flowing river, taking to the trail that would follow the Bitterroot river upstream into the long valley that lay in the shadow of the Bitterroot mountains.

Four more days of monotonous travel, each night the same, the days marked by the brilliant colors of the early fall and fair weather, but the continuous rhythm of the horses' gait had become tiresome for the little ones and their fussing affected the mood of the group. But the end of the fourth day brought them through the valley that lay above the usual winter camp of the Salish, familiar country, and as they made camp that night, they knew this was the last night on the trail, and hopefully tomorrow would get them home.

As the day broke with the blazing orb glaring into the mouth of the valley, they were on the trail, anxious to get home. As they passed the site of the Salish village, the emptiness of valley with abandoned rings that once held hide lodges, the silence of the morning where there had always been the chatter of children, and the stillness of the trail brought a touch of lonesomeness to the passersby, but they knew it would soon hold the familiar faces of friends and they pushed on toward home.

They were pleased to see the valley was green, although the muted green of early fall. They had expected to see everything dry and brown, but the colors showed evidence of late summer showers that renewed life in the valley of their home. The aspen were not as gold as further north, but as the cold moved lower, the quakies would show more color. As it were, the first touch of gold still shone bright in the mountain valleys and swales that held the aspen and the oak brush and berry bushes were blushing with the pale pinks that would soon blossom into brilliant reds. Patches of late-blooming yellow flowers like the orange sneezeweed, primrose, and the arrowleaf, showed bright against the dark timber that rose from the edge of the valley.

A herd of elk were feeding on the grass in the valley bottom, and a few lifted curious heads as the family and all their horses passed on the distant trail. The valley was about six or seven miles across and the elk would return to the black timber before dark, making their beds on the thick pine needles that carpeted the woods. Gabe commented, "It's good to see the elk herdin' up, should make it easy to bag a few for our winter supply."

"I'd like to find some laggard buffalo that haven't started south yet, reckon there'd be any further down?" asked Ezra, thinking how good a nice hump roast would taste, smothered with gravy and potatoes, washed down by a pot of coffee.

"Might be, we'll hafta check that out."

"I'd like to get a moose!" declared Cougar. Her favorite meat had always been moose and to have one hanging for the winter would please her immensely. She smiled at the thought.

"One thing I don't want, is bear!" announced Dove. "The grease is alright, but I'll eat just about anything instead of bear!"

"Do we need to get a bear for the grease?" asked Gabe, "or do we have enough?"

Cougar frowned, "We will have to look at the supply. I think we had some left, but if it is still good, I do not know."

"All this talk of meat 'n such has got me hungry. I know we wanna get home, but these horses are plum wore out and we could use a good meal," suggested Ezra.

"There's a spot up there we've used before, should be fine for a rest stop," offered Gabe, pointing to a stand of ponderosa that shaded a small clearing.

They put into the site, slipped from their horses, and soon had a fire going to heat up the leftovers from the morning's meal of strip steaks and biscuits. Ezra was quick to fill the coffee pot with spring water and sat it on the flat rock beside the fire. They had loosened the girths on the horses, dropped the travois from the buckskin, and let the group wander, leads trailing to keep them near.

As they sat munching on their warmed-over steak biscuits, Gabe caught movement down the tree line, sat his biscuit down and reached for his rifle as he stood to get a better look. He waited a moment, watched, then said, “There’s your bear grease!” and brought the rifle to his shoulder. Cougar stood and went to Gabe’s side, looking at the edge of the trees to see the dark fur of a black bear moving from the trees and into the valley, probably bound for the berry bushes that grew beside the river. Gabe was lifting his rifle as he asked, “Do you want it?” meaning the winter’s supply of bear grease. He waited for a response, then felt a hand on the barrel of his rifle, pushing it down as Cougar Woman said, “Not that one.”

Gabe frowned, looked at his woman, then to the bear and saw two more coming from the trees, smaller than their mother, the cubs were running to catch up, humping and running as fast as they could, but the mother did not slow her stride to wait for them, although she was heard to bark and growl at them, prompting them to quicken their pace.

“What do you suppose she said?” asked Gabe, his rifle at his side.

Cougar laughed, “Hurry up kids ‘fore that man shoots you!”

Gabe dropped his rifle down, placing the butt on his foot and standing with his hands layered over the muzzle. He placed his chin on his hands and stood still, looking at the wide valley beyond. This was home country, a sight he would never tire from taking it in, a wonder that he was here, with a wonderful woman, two children, and great friends. He glanced to heaven, spoke a silent prayer of thanksgiving, and smiled at his woman as she stepped close beside him.

The last leg of their journey saw them make the turn into their valley, the two long ridges pointing into the valley and marked their home. The trail cut through the trees then followed the tree line on the north edge, staying in the grass as the trail pointed to the lower lake. As they passed the lake, Gabe pointed out sign of moose grazing and thrashing through the brush, garnering a smile from Cougar Woman. When the trail bent into the trees and did its switch back, the trees seemed to envelope them in a welcome home hug, and each one could be seen taking a deep breath of the pine scented mountain air.

The trail crested the slope and bent toward the cabin, riding the shoulder, and pushing through the trees. As Gabe broke from the timber, he reined up and let the others come alongside. They stared at the cabin, surprised at what they saw. Ezra muttered, "Another grizz!"

"Ummhmm," answered Gabe, slowly shaking his head. He spoke to Ezra, "You take the uphill side, I'll go the other way," as he reached for his rifle and swung down from his saddle. He looked at Cougar as he handed Bobcat to his mother, then started toward the cabin. They would have to make sure it was clear, knowing it would not be surprising to see the bear take the cabin for his own or at least to break into the cavern which served as their cold storage for meat and supplies.

The men looked at one another, nodded, and started to the cabin. Both bringing their rifles to their shoulder, muzzle down, thumbs on the hammers. They moved slowly, watching not only the cabin, but the surrounding area in case the bear would be returning. They came to the corners about the same time, Gabe watching as Ezra checked the porch, door, and front window. Shutters had been ripped off, claw marks marked the logs, but the door was secure. The dark interior showed little from the front window. Then with a nod, Ezra went to the side.

They moved along the sides of the cabin, seeing more shutters on the ground, but no evidence the bear had entered the cabin. At the back where the cabin butted up to the cliff and the entry to the cavern, the logs, reinforced since the last break in by a grizzly, stood firm. Relieved, the men came back to the front, stepped to the porch and Ezra watched as Gabe worked on the wood dowels that held the two cross bars in place. After twisting and pulling, he freed the cross bars, sat them aside, then pulled the latch string to open the door. He pushed it in, letting the sunlight bathe the floor and show the dusty and musky interior. Gabe stepped in, looking around, then told Ezra, "Looks fine. He didn't get in this time!"

It took a while to open things up, clean it out and make ready for the gear to be brought in and the youngsters allowed inside. While they worked, the youngsters played on the buffalo robes on the porch, watched over by Wolf. The men tended the horses, rubbing them down before turning them into their home pasture. Ebony led the way, tossing his head, and taking off at a run, bucking, kicking, and twisting in the air. "I think he's glad to be home!" declared Gabe, laughing at the big stallion.

"Aren't we all?" answered Ezra, watching his big bay follow Ebony to the upper end of the pasture. The other horses trotted after, none looking back at the men. Gabe and Ezra turned back, stacked the gear and tack in the tack shed, then went to the house. The women had finished with their once-over cleaning and the little ones were happily playing on the blanket on the floor, the women watching over them as they sat at the table.

When the men walked in, they took a seat at the table with the women and Ezra asked, "What's for supper?" grinning as he looked at Dove.

"I dunno. What'chu fixin'?" she asked, making everyone laugh as much at the question as that they were relieved to be home at last.

33 / HOME

Both men had their own spots for their morning time with the Lord, and both were on the upper shoulder of the long ridge, facing the morning sun, yet sitting in the shade of a tall tree. Gabe had made a log bench that enabled him to lead against a tall spruce and watch the sun rise. Ezra had picked a spot in a stack of lichen covered limestone, fashioning himself a seat padded with dry moss and offering a back rest against another rock, while a scrubby cedar offered ample shade as it held tenaciously to a long crack in the rocks.

The grey line of first light gave way to the hint of pink as the sun pushed up from behind the distant mountains, painting the hazy sky with brighter colors, sending lances of color high above, announcing the arrival of another day. The brilliance of the rising sun bent its rays over the mountain top, stretching long shadows before it, letting Gabe and Ezra watch as the distant valley, and the narrow valley below them, came alive with the golden touch of sunshine. It promised to be a good day.

As they gathered at the table for breakfast, Ezra had a broad smile as he smelled the coffee and the baking cornbread, he grinned at his wife and took her hand, "Ummmm. Sure smells good!"

"Sure does," echoed Gabe, smiling at Cougar.

She came to him, sat on his lap, and said, "Then pray about it!"

Gabe gladly led the family in prayer, thanking the Lord for the many blessings and the food before them. He asked for God's provision for the coming winter and protection through the cold weather. As he finished, everyone said 'Amen!' and Ezra added, "Let's eat!"

As they sat together, enjoying the meal at the table, the children snoozing on the blankets, they discussed what needed to be done to prepare for the coming winter.

"With the house in good shape, I reckon all we need to do is lay in some meat," stated Gabe.

"And the hides must be cleaned and prepared also," replied Cougar. "Perhaps Dove and I should do the hunting, you two tend the children and fix the hides," pointing to the men with her chin, keeping a sober expression as she spoke.

Gabe looked at Cougar, then to Ezra and said, "Hmmm, so you want to go out into the woods with that grizzly that tried to get into the house, kill an elk or moose, drag it around and gut it, lift it up on a pack horse, and haul it back, getting all bloody and tired in the doing of it. Is that right?"

"Well, all you would have to do is nurse the babies, clean their bottoms when they make a mess, and wash their clothes. While they sleep you have to fix the food for our meals, then clean their bottoms again, and again, wash their clothes again, and clean up their messes. And when we come home with bloody hides, you must stake them out, scraped them clean, and stretch them, cover the hides with a slurry made from the brains, using just your hands, and then stretch them on a rack. But if the little ones mess their britches, you have to stop what you are doing and tend to them. Then start over again, and again, and again."

Gabe looked at Ezra, "Nah, we'll stick to huntin'," and the men nodded together.

It was a good time as they shared and laughed together and kidded one another. Each one knowing the duties of the other, but also knowing all the work would be shared by one and all.

When they left the cabin, both men trailed a pack animal, Ezra with the mule and Gabe with the big grey, and they started for the lower end of the Big

Hole basin, hoping for some buffalo. It was not unusual for some stragglers to stay behind when the bigger herds started their migration to southern country and warmer climates. When Gabe and Ezra came from the mouth of their canyon, they turned to the south, headed for the valley that marked the end of the long line of the Bitterroot mountains.

It was late morning when they neared the south end of the basin and took to a long finger ridge that was bald on the north slope, but timbered on the south. Gabe knew the big grassy flat on the far side was a favorite graze of the migrating buffalo and might hold any stragglers. As they neared the crest of the ridge, they stepped down, ground tied the animals and bellied down at the crest. Both men grinned as they spotted the dark brown bulks of a small herd of buffalo, probably twenty in the bunch, mostly cows with calves, but a few young bulls and cows without calves. Ezra whispered, "Just what we wanted!"

Gabe watched, looking at the surrounding terrain, then pointed to the end of the long meadow where another finger ridge jutted out to block off the flat, and suggested, "Wait till I get around that point. You can move down through the trees here and take the first shot. If they move that way, I'll be there to take another'n. If they don't, I'll come around and take one."

"Sounds reasonable," answered Ezra, "My mouth's

already waterin' for a nice buffler steak!"

Gabe grinned, crabbed his way down from the crest and stepped aboard Ebony. It took no more than a quarter hour to get to his point and he had just stepped down and started for the tree line when he heard Ezra's shot. He stepped around the trees, looked at the herd, saw them start his way, but just at a walk. He waited a few moments, heard another shot from Ezra, and the herd started at a run toward the trees where he waited. Gabe stepped beside a big spruce, brought the hammer to full cock to set the triggers and lifted the rifle to his shoulder. He searched the rumbling mass of brown for a target, preferring a young bull or a cow without a calf. As they drew near, he picked his target and lined up his sights, waiting for them to get a little closer. As the herd rumbled through the grass, he picked his target and squeezed off his shot. The Ferguson bucked and blasted, spitting smoke and lead, and Gabe leaned against the tree, starting the reloading process by feel as he watched the animals swerve away from the trees and saw his targeted bull stumble and fall, sliding on his chin, his feet under his chest.

The rest of the herd rumbled past and Gabe finished reloading the rifle and with a quick look around, started for the downed animal. He looked back toward where he thought Ezra would be and saw his friend standing beside a brown carcass, waving at him. Gabe waved back, poked the downed bull to be certain he was dead and was startled when the beast snorted and shook his head, coming to his feet. The bull stumbled as he stood, shook his head again, and blew blood and snot from his nose, mouth hanging open, beard almost touching the ground, and a low rumble came from his deep chest.

Gabe had stepped well back from the beast, surprised that he was still alive, and watched as he came to his feet. But when the bull turned to look at him, Gabe fired the Ferguson from his side, the bullet taking the beast in the neck, dust puffed, and blood showed. The bull staggered to the side, trying to turn to face the threat and stumbled again. Gabe instantly spun the trigger guard on the Ferguson, opening the breech, grabbed a patched ball from his bag, and jammed it in the breech, snatched at his powder horn to pour powder into the breech, all while keeping his wide eyes on the bull, as it stumbled about, blood and snot spraying with every breath and bellow. The animal staggered like a drunk full of home brew, unable to take more than one step and never in the same direction as the previous step.

Gabe spun the trigger guard to close the breech, fed powder to the pan, and snapped the frizzen shut as he lifted the rifle again. The bull dropped his head, making Gabe think he was going to his knees, but he pawed at the ground, throwing dirt high behind him, snorted, and started to charge. Gabe had his rifle cocked and ready, but knew a bullet to the skull would do no good, and he made several steps to the side, his feet tangling up in the tall grass, and as the bull lunged forward, Gabe fell to the side, but dropped the hammer and the rifle exploded, the bullet driving into the bulls shoulder and into his chest. The big beast stumbled again, appeared to lean to the side, and fell to the ground.

Gabe was on his back as he watched the bull fall. He struggled to his feet, watching the bull for any movement, slipped his pistol from his belt and stepped closer. As he stood near the hump of the animal, the beast let out a snort, startling Gabe and he shot the bull behind his ear. He looked at the beast, saw no movement, poked it with the barrel of the rifle and certain it was dead, Gabe plopped to the ground on his rump and sat looking at the massive brown carcass.

Ezra rode up aboard his bay, leading the mule, and sat with arms crossed leaning on the pommel of his saddle and said, "Hard to kill, huh?"

Gabe looked up at Ezra, shrugged, "You might say that."

When they came into the clearing before the cabin, pack animals loaded, hides behind the saddles, the men walking and leading the animals, the women greeted them. Cougar said, "Another lazy day hunting, huh?"

"You might say that," answered Gabe, looking at a smirking Ezra.

"Yeah, but it's good to be home though, ain't it?"

Gabe grinned, nodded, and led the animals to the cabin to start unloading the first of the meat for their winter stores. But they would be ready for whatever old man winter brought. Warm and cozy in their cabin. Home for the winter.

A LOOK AT: SAWATCH SKIRMISH (STONECROFT SAGA 13)

What started as a visit to the families of the women turned into a fight with renegade Apsáalooke warriors. But that was just the beginning of the battles…

After a friendly encounter with the Yapudttka Ute, their journey would take them into the middle of a fight between the Mouache Ute and an expedition of gold hungry Spaniards. The prospectors traveled across the southern tier of the land known as New Spain in search of the Seven Cities of Cibola – the same cities of gold once sought by Coronado – now thought to be in the headwaters of a river in the Sawatch mountains of the Rockies.

When the leader of the Spaniards tries to enslave the band of Utes to dig for gold, it starts a bloody battle. But when Gabe and company learn about captives and the treatment of them as slaves that does not sit well with Ezra who will fight any form of slavery wherever it is found.

Blood will fill the sluice boxes and rivers of the Sawatch Range before this conflict is over!

ABOUT THE AUTHOR

Born and raised in Colorado into a family of ranchers and cowboys, B.N. Rundell is the youngest of seven sons. Juggling bull riding, skiing, and high school, graduation was a launching pad for a hitch in the Army Paratroopers. After the army, he finished his college education in Springfield, MO, and together with his wife and growing family, entered the ministry as a Baptist preacher.

Together, B.N. and Dawn raised four girls that are now married and have made them proud grandparents. With many years as a successful pastor and educator, he retired from the ministry and followed in the footsteps of his entrepreneurial father and started a successful insurance agency, which is now in the hands of his trusted nephew. He has also been a successful audiobook narrator and has recorded many books for several award-winning authors. Now finally realizing his life-long dream, B.N. has turned his efforts to writing a variety of books, from children's picture books and young adult adventure books, to the historical fiction and western genres.

Made in the USA
Monee, IL
09 August 2021